GORILLA GUERRILLA

GORILLA
GUERRILLA

a novel by
Nick Taussig

BOOKS

REVOLVER BOOKS

Published by Revolver Entertainment

Revolver Entertainment Ltd, 10 Lambton Place, Notting Hill Gate, London W11 2SH

First published in Great Britain in 2008 by Revolver Books, an imprint of Revolver Entertainment Ltd, Registered Offices: Craven House, 16 Northumberland Avenue, London WC2N 5AP

ISBN: 978-1-905978-11-3

Cover design © Rachael Evitt 2008

A CIP Catalogue record for this book is available from the British Library

Text design and typesetting by Dexter Haven Associates Ltd, London
Printed and bound by Mackays of Chatham Ltd, Chatham, Kent

www.revolverbooks.com

This book is dedicated to
Ojok Charles

Preface

The African country I write about in this novel is anonymous. The human protagonist, Kibwe, is conceived in a similar vein. To this end, I have liberally borrowed words from numerous languages. A glossary follows this preface.

I am also non-specific about the subspecies of gorilla I write about. Primatologists reading this book might see in Zuberi, the non-human protagonist, a hybrid of mountain and eastern lowland gorilla, reflected in the description of his environment, his behaviour and his dietary preferences.

Glossary

Aka	AK-47 assault rifle
banda	mud and thatch hut
bilulu	insects
blackjack	widely distributed weed with barbed black seeds
boda-boda	motorcycle taxi
Dombeya rotundifolia	wild pear tree
Faurea saligna	African beech tree
Gorilla beringei	the Eastern Gorilla, a species of the genus Gorilla
Hagenia abyssinica	African redwood tree
hootseries	silverback vocalisation consisting of prolonged distinct hoo-hoo-hoos
kidogo	child soldier
liana	woody climber
Mai Mai	community-based militia groups active in DR Congo
matoke	green plantain

muzungu	white man
panga	machete
pombe	banana beer
posho	maize flour or ground maize and water
Pygeum africanum	African cherry tree
simsim	sesame seeds
sorghum	cereal crop
sumu	black magic or poison
tembo	elephant
Vernonia galamensis	plant in the sunflower family, often known as ironweed

Like violent apes, covered in our own blood, we long for reassurance

FRANS DE WAAL

Any animal whatever, endowed with well-marked social instincts ... would inevitably acquire a moral sense or conscience, as soon as its intellectual powers had become as well developed, or nearly as well developed, as in man

CHARLES DARWIN

Drawn Threads

Sorry cannot undo
the stitches of the past,
however strong the will.

Long hands stretch back and forth
across six million years
of weaving evolution.

Still eyes beyond green fronds
catch in the tapestry
of frozen watchfulness.

Shawls of cartridge cases
swaddle the soul and sear
tight scars across the heart.

Why do we forget
it is wrong to steal
another life?

Christine Rose

part

1

The sound of a voice wakes me.

I am still tired, it is black outside, it must be the middle of the night.

I am not with my mother and father, no, but with my friend, Oleé. His mother has gone to the town for a few days, she is sick, has the disease, the one that you get from being bad, even though she is good. She needs to get medicine to make her better, and I said I would stay with him while she is away. He is a year younger than me, he is nine, and does not like to be on his own, not because of his age but because he is scared, like all of us are, scared of *them*.

Oleé kneels over me, shaking me and speaking. He says, 'Come on, we must go, they are here.'

'How do you know?' I mumble.

'I can hear them. Listen.'

Sitting up, I concentrate on my ears, hear nothing, then see him lift the curtain to the banda and step outside. 'Come on,' he says again.

I follow him, but as I reach the curtain and make to leave as well I am pushed back in by two pairs of hands, which seem to come from nowhere, out of the darkness. I fall hard on my bottom, then on my back, the straw mats not cushioning my fall, and the back of my head goes thud as it thumps against the hard ground.

I try and see their faces, but I cannot, because there is a big bright light being shined at me, so bright it makes me feel dizzy, and I must shield my eyes with my hands to stop the light getting in.

Smack...smack, one of them punches my face, I feel his knuckles sink into my cheek, then the other one kicks me hard in the side, in the ribs. I shout, 'Get off!'

'Shut up! Be quiet!' one of them demands, his voice sounding young like mine, and I feel something rigid and cold on the side of my forehead, just above my eye, and so I look up and see that it is a gun, a big one, I do not know its name, the barrel pressed hard against my skin, in the place where if you push hard enough your eyeball will just pop out. This is what my father told me, and I imagine this now and hope that it will not.

Then the other one shines the torch at me again and hisses, 'If you shout once more, we'll kill you.' His voice is deeper, I notice. He points a gun at me as well, making me look right up its barrel and into its blackness, and this frightens me a lot.

And so I am quiet now, say nothing.

The one with the younger voice drags me to my feet and ties my hands with rope behind my back, pushes me out of the banda, then says, 'Start walking, and do not try and run away.'

I begin to walk, and then find myself being pulled backwards, which makes me almost fall over again on my bottom, and I realise that he has me on a lead like a dog, even though I am a human being.

Walking through the camp now, the place where we have lived since they came three years ago and forced us out of our homes in the villages, I see that they have taken some other boys as well, and some girls. They also have lots of our food. They must have raided the grain store. Though I can see almost nothing because it is so dark, other than their torch lights flickering in the night, I hear the screams of grown-ups. They are killing them again like they did before, with pangas rather than guns, just hacking off their arms and legs. If they use guns the government soldiers will hear them more easily and come and get them and make us safe again. But no government soldiers have come tonight.

When we get outside the camp we are herded together like animals. Some of the others they have taken are smaller than me, and some bigger. The tallest of them counts us. We are twelve, nine boys and three girls. He grunts, which makes him sound like a pig, then says, 'Give them the food to carry.'

'Yes Captain!' says the one with the deeper voice who took me, and then each of us has one of the sacks of sorghum, beans and groundnuts taken from our store put on our heads. We cannot carry them in our arms because our hands are still tied behind our backs.

'Make sure you do not drop them,' the man they call Captain warns us, a tall skinny man of about twenty-five, with a nose that is too big, and eyes that are too small, for the rest of his face. He finishes with, 'Let's go,' and we start to walk off, into the black of the bush night.

2

It is midday and I lounge in the sun.

I feel rather restless, however, and so get to my feet, pace up and down, then stomp around, breaking off branches and beating my chest as hard as I can. I wonder if my pok-poks will ever be as loud as my father's.

After this display I look straight to him, my father, Kitwiti, to see if he has noted it. He has, and nods his head in recognition.

I am so excited by his acknowledgement, so proud, that I exchange vocalisations with my siblings, these carrying throughout the forest. I wish that I were old enough to make hootseries: when I reach twelve I will be able to, and then I really shall be like him.

This green, lush and heavy forest we live in, rich with the different smells of the vast array of vegetation and the cacophonous sounds of dazzling birds, I love it here.

I lounge once more, lying on a bed of leaves.

The air is balmy, moving slowly, carried by a gentle breeze. I yawn noisily as I watch a giant butterfly flit from one flower to the next; it is the size of a small bird. Then I hear the call of an African broadbill.

∞

There are fifteen of us. Our group consists of one silver-back, my father, four mature females, the eldest of them my mother, four young adults, of whom I am one, three juveniles and three infants.

I love days like this, spent together as a family resting and feeding in the sunshine, the forest floor like a great bowl of heat and light, the air warm and sweet. We gorillas thrive in the sun, as does the whole forest around us, flowers turning their heads to meet its bright glare and creepers climbing trunks in order to get closer to its rays.

Two juveniles, my half brothers, rough-and-tumble play: they roughhouse wrestle, then chase one another and race-climb trees, the air full of their hoarse play chuckles. Sadly, I am too big now for such shenanigans, otherwise I would join them.

When I was an infant and a juvenile I wanted to fool around and have fun all the time. Young gorillas are very playful. Me and the other youngsters used to hurl our-selves in the air, performing clumsy acrobatics – twirling, spinning, kicking and chest-patting – and when we were not doing this we would climb mtanga-tanga trees and knock their fruit to the ground, which invariably ended up hitting one of the grown-ups on the head as they hurtled, like miniature missiles, towards the forest floor.

My father used to play with me when the others would not: he is very patient and tolerant. He would sometimes show his affection by picking me up by the scruff of my neck, out of the embrace of my mother, Likasi, grooming me, then returning me to her stomach. And yet he always did this with such gentleness. At first sight humans would suppose my father is incapable of being quite so gentle – his massive body seems not to permit it – and yet they would be wrong. Brute force and tenderness co-exist in gorillas in perfect harmony.

∞

It is late afternoon now, and the strong bright light of earlier has faded to a softer yellow. We continue to laze in the sun. My younger sister, Lisala, a beautiful infant with big brown eyes, seems very happy, held lovingly in my mother's arms. She makes soft purring sounds like a leopard at rest.

Then my father belches, and we all join him, the entire family, a chorus of belchers. Even Lisala accompanies us, and I recognise her right away, her vocalisations are so distinctive: I have always been able to hear her above the other females in the group, even my mother, who has a powerful voice.

∞

With sunset we start to prepare our nests for the night, grouped around my father, the forest closing in, the riotous green dying away and the vast creepers, which festoon the trees, seeming to dominate now, as if their perpetual growth has shut out the light. We feel safe. We will sleep well tonight.

3

As I walk I start to lose feeling in my body, and my ears seem blocked, every noise sounding muffled, like everything has slowed down. Maybe this is because I am so full of fear.

Oleé is not with us, I notice, he must have got away.

The smallest boy, who walks behind me, starts to cry. I know him, he is in my clan, his father is a kind man. The boy is no more than six or seven.

His crying gets louder. I turn round and tell him he must stop, otherwise they will do something bad to him. But he carries on until Captain finally loses his temper and shouts, 'Bring that boy here!'

The boy is dragged, kicking and screaming, out of the line and over to him. Captain pulls out a small gun, it is called a handgun I think, and puts it to the boy's head. 'You were told to be quiet,' he says coldly, and then making sure we are all watching, he pulls the trigger...bang!

The boy's knees immediately give way, and he collapses. I watch his head bleed onto the ground until there is a big red pool, which seeps into the dust and dirt.

Captain is silent for a moment, next looks up and says, 'Anyone else who makes as much noise will also die.'

'You hear Captain Djeke?!' another one of them shouts.

We all answer, 'Yes,' and then I whisper the Lord's Prayer to myself, say it very quickly, two times, and hope that it will protect me.

∞

We march in one long line until we reach another group of them. They did not raid the camp with the others. They are just waiting here to meet us, and are mainly young boys like me, about my age, a few of them a bit older. One man stands beside them, like he is keeping guard.

Captain greets them with the words, 'We have done well, we have more recruits, and food for tonight,' then says, 'but for now we must move straight on, the bastards will be following us.'

The young boys in this group are made to carry things like we are, though not food but rather big metal crates. I do not know what is inside them. I also see two boys carrying an older boy on a stretcher, who looks like he is sixteen or seventeen. I listen to him as we walk. He moans a bit when he is awake, and sounds like he is in a lot of pain, but when he is asleep he is completely silent, and I wonder if he has just stopped breathing.

We seem to walk for a long time, through the dark and into the morning and then the afternoon. I do not know where we are going, but we are going deep into the bush.

Finally we come to what looks like a camp, though it does not have mud huts, but just two tents and some lean-tos.

'Put the food over there!' Captain orders us, pointing towards a group of women and girls who sit round a fire, moths skittering around in the light it gives off. 'They will prepare the food.'

Next he calls to the other boys, 'Porters! Ammo and medical supplies over here,' and he motions towards a spot underneath a large tree where other big metal crates sit.

And lastly, he shouts, 'Line up! Commander Kalango will see you now,' and when he says this name everyone is quiet, and I can feel the fear in the air because it is suddenly so still.

∞

A man walks towards us, he is my father's age, thirty-five. He is very tall and has a fat belly. He wears a full army uniform, all green except for his boots, which are leather and as black as the night.

He stops right in front of us, puts his hands on his hips, then smiles, his massive white teeth shining – there is a big gap between the front two – and the whites of his eyes flashing in the dark green of the forest. Like Captain, he does not have a big gun or machete, just a handgun.

Slowly he walks down the line, inspecting each of us in turn, all eleven of us, clicking his tongue, which makes his big fat cheeks wobble up and down like the blubber on a pig's belly, and punching his open palm. He does these two things a lot, like he cannot stop doing them. When he gets to me, he stands still, looks down at me.

I am frightened to look up at him, so I quickly drop my head down and gaze at the ground, the thick black earth on the forest floor. He puts his massive hand under my chin, it seems as large as a giant palm frond, then lifts my head up to meet his stare. He is smiling, his eyes look kind, then he breaks out into a big laugh, ha-ha-ha-ha-ha. His whole belly shakes, and he pats it proudly with both hands as if it is his best friend. I would not be this proud if I was as fat as him.

He carries on down the line until he reaches the girls at the end. Two of them are my age, but one is a bit older, maybe twelve or thirteen. He strokes the cheek of the eldest, then puts one hand on her bosom, the other on her thigh. She pushes his hands away, saying, 'Do not touch me there!'

Captain steps forward now and shouts angrily, 'What are you doing, girl? Commander Kalango can do what he likes to you!' And with these words he slaps her hard across the cheek.

The Commander says quietly, his voice deep like a giant boar's, 'This one has spunk. Bring her to me later!'

He does not pay much attention to the other two girls, then turns round and walks slowly back down the line, pointing at different boys as he goes. I do not know what this means, but I count the number of times he does this, four times, and I am one of the boys he points to.

When he gets to the end he says, 'Let's keep these four. The rest, they can go. Send them back to the camp.'

'Come here!' Captain calls to them, the ones who have not been pointed to. 'You boys, you are too old,' he says to them. 'We do not want you. You go home and tell your families we have spared you. And take these two girls with you. They are no good to us.'

The six of them stand there for a moment, not knowing what to do, before Captain hisses, 'Shoo. Go on, Shoo! What did I say?!' He spits at their feet, thwuh… thwuh, does this twice, hard and fast, next flings his arms in the air and shouts, 'Go! Go!'

And then they are suddenly gone, all of them, turning and scampering off into the bush, back from where we have come. I have no idea if they will be able to find their way. I hope so.

Captain then turns to us and looking at the Commander he says sternly, 'I'll have them killing in no time.'

⊘

They like boys my age, I know this, grown-ups in my clan told me that this is because it is easier to get them to do what they want, become like them. But I am not going to become like them, do bad things like they want me to do, I say to myself.

'Tomorrow, we head north, but for now, you sleep,' Captain says. Our hands are still tied together as he tells us to lie down on a patch of grass nearby and orders the older boy with the deeper voice who abducted us from the camp to keep guard, and make sure we do not run away.

The older boy says to us as Captain walks away, 'If you try and escape we will find you, and if we do not find you then the spirits will, and they will curse you and you will die.'

As I lie down I feel very hungry, can smell the food that the women and girls have cooked, but they do not give us any. They do not care. I listen to all of them as they laugh and joke while they eat. I try not to think about my stomach, which rumbles and squelches like a sick frog because it is so empty. Instead I start to focus on the pain on the soles of my feet. I inspect them. They are swollen and bloody. They took us from our beds, did not even allow us to fetch our sandals. I worry how I will be able to carry on walking through the bush barefoot. I would wrap them in banana leaves if I could. I stare at the older boy who stands guard over us now, leaning against a tree with his big gun pointed to the ground. He wears green gumboots, as do the rest of them, except the Commander, who has his leather boots, which are as black as the night. I finally find the courage to ask when we will get boots. The older boy says nothing at first, just stares at me, then walks over and gives me ten hard strokes with the butt of his gun. This hurts a lot and makes me cry. When he has finished he says, 'You will get them from the first government soldier you kill. This is how I got mine.'

It is not easy to sleep on the grass without a blanket, it is cold, and so I lie on my side, bring my knees up to my chest and curl up in a ball to try and get warm. The other boys sleep next to me, and during the night we cram together, using each other's bodies for warmth. But I find it very difficult to sleep, because the sadness I feel will not go away. I worry what has happened to my mother and father, and I worry what will happen to me. Also I find it hard, because the boy next to me makes whining noises, like he is having lots of nightmares, and I think about waking him so he will not have to suffer any more, but I do not.

I lie there wide awake and listen to the noises on the night air, then look over at the bigger boys, the Seniors, the ones who have guns. They have shelter under the lean-tos and sleep near a big burning fire, so they are warm, not like us. The crackle of the fire is noisy, I watch its leaping orange flames. A boy stands over it with a big palm frond and uses it like a giant fan, waving all the smoke away. If the government soldiers see the smoke then they could come and rescue us.

Next I look over at the two tents, just beyond the Seniors, their green canvases illuminated by the fire. I watch the Commander go into one of them. He holds the hand of the girl from my camp. At the same time I hear other women's and girls' voices coming from the second tent, which must be Captain's. They have many wives.

4

We are on the move in the cool early morning sun, through a bamboo zone, when my father first spots him…a lone silverback. He is after my mother and aunt, Chim, and attempts to herd them away from the rest of the group. Silverbacks often come to blows, and will fight vigorously to preserve their harem and defend their territory. Humans often judge such encounters to be the mark of a primitive species, and yet they are, surely, no different from the wars that humans wage amongst themselves.

I do not feel frightened. For I know that my father will see off this challenger with short shrift. My father is very large, over two hundred kilograms, significantly bigger than the average mature male, and when he stands up on two legs he is some six feet tall.

Initially he just watches while the young pretender first attempts, rather clumsily, to herd them – though it is clear my mother and aunt have no intention of going with him – then looks to display his strength, which he does unconvincingly, flattening the vegetation in front of him and ripping giant bamboo from the earth. He is preparing himself for a confrontation with my father. But this strutting and posturing is almost comical. It is a bluff display that I am certain will not descend into violence.

Only when he has finished does my father arch his back, push his chest out and tense his massive pectoral muscles, and hold his head high. He averts his gaze first, then stares hard into his challenger's eyes – determined to retain absolute breeding rights with my mother and the other three adult females in the group – and I watch now as this younger male takes in the sheer size of my father, observing first his legs, next his arms, then his shoulders, and finally his head and sagittal crest, and it is clear to him, as he stares at his enormous form, that he is no match for my father, and so he does not meet his stare, but rather just turns and runs, carving out a virgin flee route through thick bamboo.

My father did not even have to bare his canines, I realise, and I admire him now as he stands on the main trail through the zone – the magnificent silvering of his saddle extending across his back; the heavy scarring on his head and back, like an old warrior – and hope that one day I shall be like him. A blackback, I am not far off becoming a silver, and a few years from now I will have to leave my father, my mother and the rest of my family and go in search of other females in order to establish my own harem and, ultimately, my own family.

The prospect of this, I must confess, terrifies me, though I do not let on to my siblings. They must not perceive any frailty in me. Lately my father has become increasingly prescriptive – he wants to be sure that I am ready to go it alone – and is quick to pull me up, pig-grunting at me with frustration, whenever I fail to pay due care and attention to his instruction. He, of course, wants his eldest son to do as he has done – to raise a family, and lead and care for it with constant strength and devotion. I cannot help but feel the weight of his expectation. And even if I do manage to have my own family I know that my generation will suffer even greater human incursion. Homo sapiens poses an increasing threat to my species' survival, despite the protestations of my father, who believes that humans' ultimate goodness and intelligence will prevent them from destroying us. His 'inherited wisdom', this is what he calls it, the wisdom of his species, Gorilla beringei, which precedes Homo sapiens by many millions of years, points to this essential truth. I hope this is not just my father being naively optimistic, as my mother would imply, but even if it is, then this is surely better than him being a pessimist.

I look at my father now, still standing erect on the trail, as he watches the retreat of the lone silverback. He has always demonstrated an unswerving commitment to defend his family, his group, against all comers, and I know that, sometimes, this cannot be easy for him: being in power is a stressful business, not least because your position is always being threatened, even when you are as dominant as he is. Thus, though his ulcer occasionally gives him trouble, he never discloses this. For he is reluctant to reveal any weakness, as this will only jeopardise his position. And he must demonstrate his strength not only to outsiders but also to his own, to us – his family, his group. He has four mature females that he must satisfy – they will not waste breeding time – and children that must respect him as their father and leader.

He then walks over to my mother as the morning sun becomes more intense and brings her close, wrapping his giant arms around her, holding her there, and making soft, humming belch vocalisations in her ear; and she does the same. He is devoted to my mother, she is his favourite mature female. She grooms him more than the other adult females do. Sometimes they even share a nest together, though not last night.

Next, Lisala bounds up to him and he gathers her up in his arms. She gazes at him lovingly, almost quivering in anticipation of his warm embrace, fluttering her long eyelashes. I, too, when I was much younger, an infant, loved being held by him, and every so often would even sleep beside him, and I relished this, my father holding me as he slept. In fact, the only thing I did not delight in was his loud snoring.

I am very lucky to have a father such as him, and with this thought in my heart we continue on our way through the thick bamboo as I listen for the omnipresent trickle of water in the distance. Thankfully, I have not heard the sound of humans for some time.

5

They make us get up before dawn. I watch a few of the Seniors take down the tents. I try and count all of them, the Commander, Captain, the Seniors, smaller boys like me, porters, women and girls. I get to fifty-five, but then see a few more that I missed.

We are made to walk in one long line, and like before we must carry things. I walk with heavy steps, my head hangs down. I listen for any comforting sounds, a crow's caw even, but hear nothing other than my footsteps and the steps of others. My feet are even sorer now, I feel like I am walking on burning coals.

They do not let us stop to take a break, and I feel very weak because I have not eaten. We walk by a cassava tree, and I pull off one of its leaves and chew on it, hoping that this will relieve my hunger. But it does not.

As we walk on, Captain every so often orders two boys to run, one ahead of us and one behind us, and climb a tree. Whenever he does this he shouts, 'Lookout,' and I realise this is to make sure there are no government soldiers close by. High up in the trees, the boys can see everything. 'We guerrillas are too fast and clever for them. They cannot keep up with us,' he says proudly.

My stomach really aches now, so much so that I clutch it, then rub it to try and make it better, making circles with the palm of my hand. Maybe I should not have eaten that cassava leaf. The boy who walks behind me, he is maybe a year older than me, knows I am in pain, and so hands me a root, I do not know its name, and tells me to chew on it, says that it will make me feel better. I thank him, ask him his name, and he whispers, 'Kisunga.'

And I tell him my name, 'Kibwe.'

∽

The sun is starting to set, we have been walking all day, and the four of us, the boys they abducted, are all very tired because we have not eaten anything for almost two days. We are also very thirsty. They have given us very little water. My throat feels like it is being choked. Captain suddenly appears beside us and asks, 'Are any of you tired?'

I am about to say yes, but Kisunga throws his hand on my shoulder and answers, 'No, we are all fine.'

'I didn't ask if you were fine, I asked if you were tired,' he says angrily.

'No, we are not tired,' Kisunga replies.

'No, what?!' the older boy with the deeper voice butts in.

'No, Captain,' Kisunga says quickly.

'That's better,' the older boy replies.

'Good, let us march on then,' Captain says.

When the older boy and him walk on ahead, I turn round to Kisunga and ask him why he did not tell them the truth. 'Then we could have slept,' I say to him. 'We are all exhausted.'

'If any of us had said that we were sleepy they would have let us lie down and then killed us while we slept.'

'Why are they doing this?' I ask. 'Why?'

And all Kisunga can say is, 'I do not know.'

So now I ask God why they are doing this, but He does not answer me either. Maybe He will answer me tomorrow.

☙

When it is dark we stop and make camp for the night. They finally feed us. The women and girls cook sorghum, not maize or millet, with a gravy that looks like sick, but I eat it anyway because I am so hungry, this stodge, and know that if I told them what I thought it looked like they might take it away from me and not let me eat anything, until I was just all skin and bone. They serve it in one small cup. I finish it quickly and wish that I could have more. The older boy with the deeper voice stands guard over us again. He says, 'You will not eat with the rest of us until you have been given the medicine, that is our rule. This medicine will make you strong like me.' But I know that this medicine will not make us strong but bad, will put a wicked spirit inside us. He finishes off with, 'You will all have this medicine tomorrow. Now sleep.'

∞

We are given the medicine the following morning. All of them are there. It is like a church ceremony, even though we are in the middle of the bush and there are no prayers. The four of us are told to kneel as the Commander approaches us. An older girl holds a small clay pot, and the Commander puts his middle finger in it, makes slow circles, his finger going round and round, then puts his finger, which is covered with a red, oily liquid, to the forehead of Kisunga and makes a cross, like the Cross of Jesus. 'You are one of us now, I have given you the power. You will fight with us till the end,' he says.

Then Captain adds, 'We can see you now, all the time, now you have had the medicine. Do not think that you can run away. The medicine will mean that we will always find you.'

After Kisunga, the Commander makes crosses on the rest of our foreheads, and says the same words as he does this.

The older girl leaves the side of the Commander and returns moments later with a jerrycan full of water.

Captain says, 'This water is neither from the sky, nor a well, nor a river. No, it is special water,' and with these words the Commander dabs drops on our chests, our wrists and our backs, then fills four tiny wooden vessels with the water, puts a cork in each one, and hangs these around our necks.

After the service we pack up camp, and then are on our way again, walking all day. We are made to carry crates now, they have made us porters, and the one on my head is very heavy, it is full of ammo. As I walk I feel my knees giving way, and my feet sinking deeper and deeper into the wet muddy ground. The crate is so heavy that I think my head will simply disappear between my shoulders and be lost forever. The Seniors just carry their big guns and are noisy a lot of the time, like to shout and argue with each other, but never do this when the Commander is close by, because they know they will get punished.

In the evening we eat with the rest of them for the first time, but do not get posho and beans like they do, just sorghum and gravy again. We are them now, even though I do not like to think of myself as one of them. They also give us shelter, a lean-to, which the four of us huddle under.

∽

The next morning two Seniors come to us and tell us we must bathe. Ojok, the youngest of the four of us, asks, 'Do I have to?'

And they both reply at the same time, 'If you do not we will beat you.'

We later discover they want us to bathe not only so we stay clean and healthy, but also so they can send us into camps during the day to get food. They give us T-shirts and sandals…me, Kisunga, Ojok and Okello…to make us look like normal boys, like we were before, rather than guerrillas. The sandals are too big for me, but I do not care. I am just grateful to have something on my feet.

The younger of the two boys who abducted me is called Wasswa. He is nicer than the older boy. He looks too young to be a Senior, and yet he carries a big gun like them, which he tells me is called an AK or Aka. 'Where are we going?' I ask him.

'We are heading for the headquarters,' he replies. 'I've been there just once before. That is where he is, General Mushamuka.'

I shudder when I hear this name. My mother told me that this name stands for 'everything that is wrong with the world'.

'What does he look like?' I ask.

'His skin is light brown, not black like yours or mine. He has magical powers. He can make a tree disappear, he can change into anything…a snake, a skeleton, even the President. Some say that the Devil talks through him.'

'Then why does not he change himself into the President right now, because if he does this then he will not need you and all the others to fight for him any more.'

'You must not say this,' Wasswa says firmly.

'Yes, you heard him,' the older boy with the deeper voice butts in, and hits me hard on the arm.

'Kola, you don't need to hit him,' Wasswa says.

'I'll do what I want. I'm older than you, remember,' and then Kola hits my arm many times in the same place until it feels all floppy like a dead fish. He finishes with the words, 'You are weak, you will never be a Senior like me. You will always be just a porter!'

I finally cry out, 'Stop it, just stop it, will you?!'

And this makes two of the other Seniors laugh, to see and hear me in pain. Then Kola laughs as well, which makes me shudder. Though his voice is deep his laugh is high like a hyena's. I hate the sound of it, I can feel it get right underneath my skin.

Captain whistles now, and I know that this is the command for us to set off once more. I must carry the heavy ammo crate again. I look over at the Commander and Captain. They are both grown-ups, big and strong, and yet they carry nothing.

6

In the early afternoon we stop to eat, and I immediately head for a cluster of wild celery, only to discover that my younger half brother, Kibu, has got there first: I find him chewing on a handful of stalks, which crunch crisply in his mouth. I gesture for him to move aside, but he ignores me, and continues to eat. This annoys me, for he should respect my seniority, and so I pig-grunt loudly, giving clear voice to my disapproval. Still he does not budge. And so I simply push him, hard with both arms – I have my father's temper – and he topples over onto his side, grimacing and letting out a melodramatic scream, as if I have just beaten him with my fists. He will no doubt bear a grudge for hours now, and will not rest until he gets me back.

My father bounds straight over, and rather than singling out one of us for blame he reprimands us both, snapping his mouth open and shut, mock-biting – his way of disciplining us, his unruly children. I immediately assume a classic submissive posture, bending down on my forearms, sticking my rump in the air and averting my gaze. He has always been a great arbiter of disputes within his family, and never fails to protect its weaker members if they are threatened by the more dominant. I wish to be like him one day, so dignified and commanding of respect, and thus I reluctantly share the cluster of celery with my half brother.

I care for Kibu, but just two years younger than me he is constantly trying to assert himself – not helped by the fact that he wishes his mother, not mine, was the dominant female in the group – reluctant to acknowledge my authority as the eldest sibling. And yet it is this very hierarchy which gives order to gorilla society, which limits intragroup conflict. I know that, even when fully grown, he will never be as large as me. For his mother is small, and he does not have my appetite. But what he will lack in stature he will compensate for in cunning. He already displays a considerable amount of this characteristic, and I imagine he will rely on it even more when he matures and is driven to establish his own group – for he will need to. In fact, I imagine that when he reaches sexual maturity he will simply ally himself with our father, support his leadership, and only take control when our father is too old, when he is confident that there will be no violent repercussions.

My father makes his way over to a Pygeum africanum nearby. He has always had a great penchant for the fruit it bears, and will go to extraordinary lengths in order to satisfy this fondness, and I laugh now as I watch him climb it, this spectacle of an enormous silverback heaving himself up the tree's thin trunk, in a rather undignified manner, transfixed by the wonderful scent of ripeness, in order to get at the fruit at the top, some sixty feet up, and filling his hands and mouth to the brim. He taught me how to seek out the ripe fruit: not only does it taste better, but it does not give you an upset stomach either.

According to my father – a very sage gorilla, he has been committed to, and thorough with, his offspring's education, particularly in respect of biology, evolutionary theory, history and politics – our early ancestors could most likely not have achieved this feat, of scaling a difficult, high tree such as this. The first primates evolved about sixty-five million years ago, and hominids, human-like apes, about seven million years ago. Homo sapiens, which evolved from these hominid species around five hundred thousand years ago, has proven itself to be the most successful of the apes, dominating the world and now living mainly in cities, in huge colonies. In fact, this particular primate species is making it difficult for Gorilla beringei to survive, and I am increasingly unsure of my father's conviction that humans' ultimate goodness will prevail, that they will not destroy us. Please, let them not return and threaten us once more.

When he finally descends the tree once his stomach has had its fill of fruit, I ask him why the process of the natural world is so callous and cruel, and he answers that though it might be this way what it produces is often the very opposite, something sympathetic and kind. I must remember this, I suppose, not least because I am prone to glumness, unlike him.

∽

We have spent the greater part of today so far searching for, and eating, food, and we continue to do this late into the afternoon. In fact, this is what we gorillas do most days. A decreasing number of humans in sub-Saharan Africa still lead a subsistence life as we do.

After we have, at long last, finished feeding ourselves we groom one another. This is our primary means of social interaction: we groom rather than speak. Language, as I am sure humans are well aware, has its limitations. The size of our groups is restricted by this, however – grooming is a time-consuming business, and it is only possible for a gorilla to groom so many members of his or her group in one day.

This afternoon, after I am done with eating celery, I groom my sister. I meticulously part her hair with my lips and fingers, removing all parasites, dry-skin flakes and vegetation debris, and I spend a good hour doing this.

Language, spreading the word, enables humans to exist in far larger social groups – thoughts, feelings and ideas can be expressed to many at the same time. And yet this benefit, I feel, does not come without its detriment:

it often complicates their relationships, because different members of their groups have opposing views about what has been said, and then force others to see things as they do. Humans also have the habit of speaking enigmatically and evasively much of the time, normally when they are reluctant to say what they really feel. However, my father forever cautions me against being too critical: better I use my knowledge to be wise and understanding rather than foolish and unsympathetic.

When my mother grooms me now, after I have finished grooming Lisala, I know she is cross with me after my earlier confrontation with Kibu: she tugs at my hair that little bit harder than usual, her frustration and disapproval clear enough, this action speaking far louder than any words she might utter if she possessed this faculty. Were my mother a human, she would most likely go to extraordinary lengths not to express her anger, but at the same time would expect me to fully know and understand how she feels.

Perhaps humans fear that without this complexity of communication they would live in a dull and intellectually impoverished world. Well…I am not so sure. The only reason why we gorillas do not speak is because our larynx is set high in the throat, just behind the back of the tongue, whereas a human's is set low: my father is always quick to point this out. It is this low position that significantly increases the resonance chamber in the throat and mouth, which makes it impossible for a human to breathe and swallow at the same time, but allows him or her to produce a vast array of sounds. And yet, because we gorillas possess a different vocal tract that limits the sounds we can make, we must rely upon our body to make ourselves heard.

I always know when my sister is sulking, as she is at this moment – because my mother continues to groom me and does not attend to her needs. She pouts, her features long and drawn out, using every muscle in her nose and face to convey her displeasure. If you could see her right now you would think she was being terribly melodramatic. And yet how else can Lisala communicate how she feels?

7

I am still very afraid after the first week, but know I must be strong if I am to survive. I need to stop thinking about my mother and father so much, though this is difficult, and whenever I try to I find that I think about them even more. They must not see me cry again, because if they do then they might just kill me.

I go on sleeping only a little each night, and have the same dream over and over, a giant snake wrapping itself around my throat and trying to strangle me. This snake is him, General Mushamuka. And every morning, when they wake us to start marching again, I must stamp my feet on the ground to try and get my legs going, get the blood into them, because they are feeling so tired and weak. But I know I must get used to this new life, for I have no other choice.

It is always hardest when we walk during the heat of the day, and they do not let us stop, even when the sun is at its hottest or when we need to relieve ourselves, so all we can do is piss in our underpants. I get very sweaty, and flies buzz around me as if they want to lick the salt and piss from my skin. If I had a free hand I would shoo them away, but I do not. My head is very itchy as well because my hair is so dirty, but I cannot scratch it.

By the end of the day I am always desperate for food, and today, this evening, after a day of heavy rain, my stomach hurts because it feels hollow, like an empty eggshell with no white or yolk inside. I am wet through as I slump down on the ground, finally getting to rest my legs. The rain was so strong today that it made the sky sound like it was belching and rumbling, as if it were angry with us or something, the noise so deep and loud that it frightened me. At one point I felt so upset that I wanted to look up and curse the sky, tell it I had had enough, was sick of it, its grey and black clouds massing and hovering, seeming to follow us wherever we walked. But then I thought maybe it was angry because of what we are doing, because we are guerrillas who do bad things.

My feet ache more than ever, as do my ankles, like they might just snap if I try and stand up again. I take off my sandals and examine my feet, like I am my own doctor, and see that some of my toes are bleeding. I have blisters on them, I count six. Next I look at my inner thighs, which are very sore as well, my wet shorts rubbing against them all day. The skin right by my thing is red raw. Earlier on I had asked Kola if I could just take my shorts off and wear my underpants, but he had said to me, 'If you are to become a man like me then you must keep them on and bear the pain.' But he is not a man yet, even though he thinks he is because he is a Senior and has a big gun. He has a small white teddy bear, he sleeps with it at night, clutching it to his chest. He likes to have his bear in one hand and his big gun in the other. He stuffs it, every morning, in his backpack, making sure no one can see him with it, though everyone knows he has it.

My shorts and underpants smell very bad. I take them off, put my T-shirt around my hips, and then wash them in a bucket with a bar of blue soap. It has stopped raining now, so I know they will dry quickly. I then put some blackjack on my legs, feet and toes: Wasswa shows me where to find this weed in the bush, and this helps soothe them a little, makes the skin softer and a little less raw.

The women and girls prepare to cook. Prosci, the girl from my camp, the one the Commander took to be his wife even though she is far too young, is sent with a few other girls to go and fetch water. She has a terrible sadness in her eyes as I watch her walk away with the others. They are followed by a Senior, to make sure none of them try and escape. The load Prosci must carry everyday is heavy like mine – a baby on her back, a large jerrycan of water on her head, and two big saucepans on her shoulders, held together by a piece of string hung around her neck, which makes it look like she is wearing an enormous ugly necklace. Her legs and feet are very swollen now. Like the other girls, she has been given a child to look after, one of the Commander's children.

We porters are ordered to go and fetch wood for the fire. They give us pangas to cut off branches. Kisunga is given an axe and told to cut down a tree. It is not easy for him to find one which is not damp and rotten after all the rain. They must be planning to make a big fire.

I dream of nice food…sweet potatoes, corn, matoke. I used to like eating, but not any more, now just eat to fill my stomach. All they give us is sorghum and that gravy, which I find out is simply boiled up cassava leaves that taste of nothing. My tummy has got big, like some of the small children's in the camp, like a giant balloon about to pop. I remember it was last like this when I was five, and my mother told me this was because of 'malnutrition', yes, that was the word she used, not enough different food in my diet, just one food which I ate all the time. That year all our crops had been destroyed by locusts, and all we had left to eat was millet. I know I would be a better porter if they gave me better food, I would be stronger. But this evening they do not, we eat the same as always. And even though I do not like it I know I must eat it, otherwise I will have no strength left. I make sure I eat it slowly, putting only a little inside my mouth each time. This is difficult to do when you are very hungry, but I must make it last.

When we are finally allowed to sleep, I lie down and dream of sleeping on a comfy mattress rather than the hard ground. Even though they have now given the four of us a blanket to share, it is still cold, and I lie awake for most of the night hoping that the sun will rise as soon as possible and there will be no more rain.

∽

The next morning we are ordered to get up early, before the birds, and told to bathe. I know right away this is because we are about to be sent on our first camp raid. I do not have a gun or machete, and am worried what will happen if I am caught. It is early morning, not night, and they will see me. But I do not have on a uniform like the rest of them, I do not look like a guerrilla, so they will not recognise me, the people in the camp, will just think that I am one of them, I hope. And yet still, I do not want to steal from them, even though I know I must.

The Commander, Captain and a few Seniors lead me, Kisunga, Ojok and Okello to the back of the camp, it is a large one, and point to a small patch of land. They are growing vegetables there, just like we did in our camp, I can see peas and potatoes.

I say to Captain, 'They are ripe, we can pick them and bring them back to you,' hoping that this will mean we do not have to go into the camp.

'No, this will take too long,' Captain says, 'I want you to go right inside. There you will find groundnuts and okra laid out on large plastic sheets on the ground. They will have left them to dry in the sun today after all the rains yesterday. Just grab one of these sheets at either end, fold it up, and then carry it straight out.'

'Yes, Captain,' I say reluctantly.

'I want you to split up,' he goes on, 'you two go in that way, and you two the other. Walk slowly, pretend you live there. And remember, we can see you all the time because of the medicine, do not forget, and if you do not come back with food then we will punish you.'

Me and Kisunga walk slowly inside. I think it is better that it is a big camp, bigger than the one we live in...were living in...because this will mean that maybe everyone who lives here does not know each other and so we will not arouse suspicion.

We soon come across a freshly picked crop of groundnuts laid out on a sheet in the early morning sun. Me and Kisunga do as Captain said, take either end and fold it up with all the nuts inside. When we do this it makes a lot of noise, the plastic ruffling and crackling, and I am sure that someone can hear us.

When we have finally folded it, we lift it up at both ends and go to run. We should have just walked. It is heavier than we think, and I stumble, drop the end I am carrying, and it spills open, nuts pouring out. I start gathering them up, throwing them back inside the sheet, but I am making a lot of noise now, I know this, and Kisunga is telling me to forget about the ones I have dropped and just carry on, and then I suddenly feel a big arm swoop over my head and grab my neck, force my head down to the ground. 'You little thief!' the voice screams. 'Guerrilla, guerrilla, I've got a guerrilla.'

I hear other voices at this moment, and the sound of more feet rushing towards me. 'I'm going to cut off your fingers. That will teach you not to steal from us!' the same voice demands.

But then there is a very loud noise, guh-guh-guh-guh-guh, the noise of an Aka, and the man holding me, the one who said he would cut off my fingers, lets go of me all of a sudden and falls down to the ground. The sound of the other feet rushing towards me stops...and then everything is silent.

Thwuh...thwuh, I hear this sound and know it is Captain. He carries an Aka, one of the Seniors' guns. He spits on the man he has shot, then hands the big gun back to the Senior to his left. 'You were lucky we were keeping an eye on you,' he says to me as I look up at him. 'Now, come!' He grabs me by my T-shirt and pulls me to my feet. 'Get the food out of here.'

As me and Kisunga go to leave once more, I turn and look at the man he has shot. Blood drips out of the corner of his mouth, and there is fear and hate in his big brown eyes as I watch him stop breathing. Captain spits at him again like he is no more than a dog.

Then I see the Commander grab another one of the men who was chasing me, force him to the ground, beat his head with the handle of his machete, then hack at him with the blade, cutting his hamstrings, then slashing his throat. 'These bastards, these collaborators, deserve to die!' he shouts.

He kills this man as if it is just a game. 'Make sure you grab some girls on the way out,' he goes on, speaking to a few Seniors. He wants more wives, he is greedy, but he does not treat them as wives but rather as animals, worse, like shit in the toilet.

Captain kicks me and says, 'Get a move on,' then says to the two Seniors who stand either side of him, 'I want us to eat well tonight. I want you two to go and kill a boar.'

∽

We return to camp with the food we have stolen, and are told that the rest of the day is for rest. I immediately go to our lean-to and lie down. I know I must try and sleep if I am to stay strong.

I close my eyes and start to think about my teacher, the one from the school in my camp not my village. He might be a small man, short and skinny, but Mr Bayona has a big brain, and he is good. He has helped me and all the other students learn many things. I miss him, my friends, I miss going to school. It seems like a long time ago that I was last sitting in front of him, in class. I wonder whether I ever will again.

I do not fall asleep, just continue to think about school. I remember how, when any of us got a question right, he would tell us to clap, to show the boy or girl how well he or she had done. He also used to get us to sing songs. He made learning fun, made us feel happy. I used to love throwing my hand in the air when I knew the answer to a question and shouting, 'Teacher!' And then I would wait for him to look at me and say in his deep voice, 'Yes, Kibwe?'

He was very good at teaching social studies, the class all about what makes a better society. They obviously have not done this class, the guerrillas, I say to myself, otherwise they would not have taken us from our homes, our families, our friends, our school, and made us do all these things we do not want to do.

The other class I loved was biology, taught by Mr Nankoma. We would learn all about the human body and where we, human beings, came from, from the great apes, the gorilla and the chimpanzee. He often made me laugh, especially when he became excited. He would stutter a little, tripping up on his words as if he just could not get them out fast enough. But he always found his way again, managed to slow down enough to speak clearly. He loved his subject.

Mr Nankoma and Reverend said different things about where we came from, and sometimes had arguments that we were not meant to hear but did. Reverend liked to talk about 'the great work the Christian missionaries from Europe' had done, how they had stopped the many different tribes from fighting each other by introducing them to the Lord. Mr Nankoma said they did the opposite, that these white men from Europe did not stop the different tribes fighting, but rather made them start. 'They might not have shared the same tribal practices, but the missionaries helped them to share a common belief in Jesus Christ,' Reverend always used to say. 'This is why Jesus is our saviour.' He did not like all the different tribal rituals and beliefs. Reverend was worried that 'since the former colonial powers had granted us independence many people were reverting to their former belief systems.' He would say to us all, 'This country needs and wants to be civilised now.' But to be honest I would often fall asleep in his classes, I found them so boring, especially because we would always read from the same book, the Bible. I never fell asleep in Mr Nakoma's though. His classes were amazing, he would always bring in different things to show us.

I open my eyes now, look out of the lean-to, and watch as the two Seniors who Captain ordered to go and kill a boar stop, huff and puff, laugh, then shout, 'Look, we got one!'

A boar lies on the ground, front and hind legs tied together, rope wound tightly round the hooves. It is a female, I can see her teats, she has a big belly, maybe she was going to have babies. Then I hear a whining noise, high and low at the same time, it is coming from her, the boar, and I realise they have not finished her off, that she is still alive.

The Commander walks over to her slowly, he holds his panga. He has that scary glint in his eye, shiny with rage, and I know that he is about to do something bad. Now, whenever he gets this look, this look of killing, we all wonder if it will be one of us. The two Seniors drag the boar to her feet, make her stand even though she is too tired and weak to after the fight she has put up. He laughs, says, 'It is pregnant, all the better,' and with these words swipes the blade of his machete across her belly. Guts and babies come tumbling out, and she screams, collapses to the ground, and the Commander roars, seeming to delight in what he has just done. She does not die right away, but moans quietly. My father has never killed an animal in this way. He always respects it to the end, even when he finally drives a spear through the heart.

There is lots of singing and dancing this afternoon as the boar is cooked, she will feed all of us, we will finally get to eat meat after a long time without. The smell of the cooking animal fills the air, the dripping of her fat thick and sweet. We must wait for the Commander, Captain and Seniors to eat before we can. I hear some of the Seniors talking. They say that the Commander wants to eat a gorilla next time, but I am not sure if I believe them. They leave us the head, not as well cooked as the rest. We must cut it off, cut out the cheeks, slice these into bits, skewer them on small pieces of wire, then hold them over the flame of the fire until they are charred on the outside and juices drip from them. I try not to think of her, how they killed her, as I eat.

Captain comes over after we have finished, and addresses me, 'The Commander's tent has a hole in it. I want you to make a shelter to go over it, to make sure no rain gets in.' He throws me his panga, which lands right by my feet. 'Do it now, before it gets dark!'

I decide to make the roof first. The grass – I use elephant grass – will need time to dry. It is the grassy season, and so the blades are nice and tall. I cut down lots, then lay them in the late afternoon sun. Next I build the main frame. I cut down strips of bamboo, make them all the same height, dig four holes in the ground, then insert four of the bamboo poles just like my father taught me. Next I build a frame for the roof, using another four poles, which I tie together with grass. I know I must make sure the roof is thick enough to stop any rain getting in. Captain warned me that 'if the Commander gets wet when he sleeps then he will be very angry' with me in the morning. So I make sure that once the stems are dry enough I bind lots of them together and make an extra-thick roof. And finally, I fix this to the top of the main frame.

The Commander comes over just as I am finishing. He is very pleased with it, and takes my hand for the first time, shakes it, then caresses it, and the tops of his fingers are fat, the skin rough and hard like dried, cured meat. I do not like him touching me.

8

The rain beats down today, a giant cascade, the patter and rush of water on leaves, the light a green-black, possessing a dark luminosity. I love it when it rains like this.

We gorillas always know when the rains are coming: we can feel them in the air, its texture becoming heavier, clammier. Humans are rather less attuned to the atmosphere, dependent upon the news of meteorologists rather than their own natural instincts. I wonder now what would happen if the rains simply did not stop.

And yet they do, finally, and it is wonderful to watch the light re-enter the forest, shafts of sunshine penetrating the trees, illuminating the giant fronds and forming glossy patches on the forest floor, the green of the vegetation becoming vivid once more.

I look over at my mother and watch her as she builds a day nest, preparing to languish in the sun for the first time today. I recall how she had taught me to build one, a night nest first, ensuring that I chose the right plants, whose leaves made for a comfortable padded base and whose stalks made for a sturdy and compact oval nest. My first attempts, poorly built feeble constructions, lasted little more than half the night. And yet I still built them, in the early evening, with great exaggerated gestures, as if I were a master nest-maker, so determined was I to prove my maturity, hide my frustration and mask my ineptitude. However, the older I got the better I became. My mother had also shown me what to do in the rainy season, to sleep in the sheltered hollow of a tree trunk, which did not require me to build a nest but rather just to lay some moss on its base. But now I am a lot bigger, I find it nigh impossible to find a trunk big enough to accommodate me, and so must rely upon no more than branches for shelter.

My father had acquired my mother first, which explains her position as the dominant female in the group. Before he entered her life, she had feared becoming a nullipara: she was desperate to give birth. I am her firstborn. Rearing offspring in our species is very demanding, as it is in Homo sapiens, requiring years of nurturing and socialisation. And like humans, we are extremely protective at first, for the first few years of the infant's life. The human brain requires nine months, next a further year before it completes its physical growth, then an additional four years before the child is mature enough to survive on its own. No wonder Homo sapiens, like Gorilla beringei, tends to pair-bond, realising it makes things a little easier if there are two parents rather than just one. We gorillas give birth every five to eight years, unlike humans, who have much shorter interbirth intervals. According to my mother, Homo sapiens' average was not far off ours, just four years, until the species devised bottle-feeding and commercial baby foods. However, despite this decreased interbirth interval, human childhood is still long. A human, just like a gorilla, needs ten to fifteen years in order to learn how to survive in his or her environment, how to fit into his or her society and follow its rules.

Today, my mother and father are funny together. While they both day nest she ridicules him as a typical male, far more concerned with the quantity than the quality of sex – yes, the male gorilla suffers from the same affliction as the male human – while she, conversely, is far more concerned about quality; to which he retorts that she has obviously chosen well then, because he is clearly the most healthy and vigorous male in the region. My mother is evidently in agreement, because she then makes a mounting solicitation, offering herself to him.

But Lisala then has a sudden outburst, sobbing and screaming – I think she feels abandoned once more – and my mother leaves my father and decides to calm her by playing peek-a-boo. I play with her as well, taking the burden off my mother, chasing her first, then gently wrestling with her. Kinship in gorilla society is very strong and durable. She was tougher on me, when I was an infant, than she is with my sister now. In fact, my mother is prone to mollycoddle Lisala, whom she encouraged to ride ventrally well beyond four months, and I sometimes worry that she will not grow up as she needs to in order to survive. And yet I realise that my mother's hard discipline was always matched by great affection. I was one of those infants who would have continued to suckle my mother well into my third year if I had been given half a chance. When she first started to refuse me I would have a temper tantrum and scream hysterically. However, she soon put a stop to this, one firm smack from her enough to make me realise that my wish for more milk would no longer be granted. But the majority of the time she did not even need to raise her hand to me to get me to comply with her wishes: it was enough that she simply snub me. This I could not bear. I would sulk and whimper until she forgave me. She has always had the perfect female's touch in this respect, preferring to turn the emotional screws rather than to use brute force. I know how fortunate I was, as an infant and a juvenile, to have a mother like her: for though she doted on me, as any loving mother inevitably does, she never let this maternal devotion affect her judgment. If I did wrong, I did wrong, and that was that.

She has an almost serene presence at this moment as she grooms Lisala. She is able to calm the whole group, often grooming members in order to settle them. In fact, the last time she was seriously perturbed was some years ago, when my brother died. He was just six months old and it hit her extremely hard. Though I was seven at the time, she began to treat me as an infant again, wanting me to be close to her at all times, even offering me her breast and inviting me to ride her dorsally, and whenever I was not with her she became sad and withdrawn. I wished she was a primiparous mother, who typically overcomes her grief through play, predominantly with juveniles in the group. However, thankfully, the subsequent conception of my sister put an end to her grief.

The other thing I admire my mother for is that she does not abuse her position as the dominant female by hogging all the food: whereas a pick of mates is my father's privilege as the dominant male, my mother's is all the food she can eat, and yet she is quite willing to share with others. And though I love her very much, I am also able to be close to the other adult females in the group: they have always been kind to me, especially my aunt Chim who, before she had her own child, would often carry me off for a whole day and nest with me, such was the pull of her maternal inclination. She used to tickle my tummy as well, which I loved. She went on to have a child of her own, a girl called Pumbu, who, just like her mother when she was a young female, is already anxious to cuddle and carry the infants in the group.

It is late, and my mother urges Lisala to rest now. She is tired and needs to sleep, and I smile as I see her watch our mother start to build a night nest: she could not hope for a better instructor. At this moment I wonder whether, all this time, I have been worrying unnecessarily. Perhaps we have finally found permanent sanctuary from them.

9

At last we reach the headquarters and he, General Mushamuka, is not there. We are told he will be with us in a few weeks. Captain summons all the porters and says, 'Now we will train you to be guerrillas. Only the toughest will make it. The rest of you will remain porters.'

I do not want to be a porter any more, I know this, do not want to carry heavy crates, do not want to be beaten all the time and called a 'big girl', this is what the Seniors call us, do not want to be treated like a mule.

There are six different tests to become a guerrilla. First, they train us to be lookouts, getting us to climb up and down trees as fast as we can. Some of the trees are very high, and they tell us that we must climb all the way to the top. Okello falls from one of them and hurts his back badly. He is taken to the sick bay. Second, they make us hold out one of our palms, put a burning coal on it, then tell us to walk twenty paces without dropping it. I smell my skin and flesh as it burns, it is a horrible smell. Ojok cries out in pain when it is his turn to do this. He manages just twelve paces. Third, each of us is ordered to guard the Commander for one full day, and we must do everything he tells us to, and do it quickly. Fourth, we are ordered to raid a village, not a camp, and steal food, and they will not be there to back us up, and we will not have any weapons. If we must fight, then we must use our 'fists and wits', this is what Captain says. I go in with Kisunga. We come across an old woman, and I am tough with her, I hold her by the neck, say, 'Where is the granary?' She is very scared and shows me right away. I take a big bag of grain, while Kisunga takes a large basin of sugar. Fifth, they teach us how to use a machete, an Aka, a PK, which is a big Aka, and an Uzi. They also show us an RPG, the gun that you must put on your shoulder to shoot because it is so big. We are also taught how to ambush, to lead the enemy into a part of the bush where we are all hiding and then jump out and attack them. And sixth, the Seniors beat us to toughen us up, we must try and remain standing, and it is Kola who is the first in line to beat me. I am in lots of pain by the time he has finished, but I do not allow myself to cry. I do not want to give him the pleasure of seeing me this way.

It is just me and Kisunga left after the six tests, the other boys including Okello and Ojok have not passed. They will carry on being porters. I feel my body is changing now, it is getting stronger, and my heart as well, it is getting harder. I hope I will not become like them. Captain comes to me and Kisunga and says, 'There are two more things you must do before you can become guerrillas. Tell them,' he says to Kola, then walks away.

Kola walks up to me, shoves his PK in my face and says, 'You must rape her,' pointing to a girl who sits on her own. She is older than me I think, about fifteen or sixteen.

I say, 'I do not know what you are talking about.'

Kola sucks air through his teeth, says back to me, 'If you are to be a Senior, then you must do it, you must make her produce. Now take off your clothes.'

I take off my T-shirt, shorts and sandals.

'Your underpants as well,' he hisses.

I stand there naked.

He continues, 'Now go and lie on top of her and put it inside, in between her legs.'

I do not know what he means. Kola walks behind me, puts his gun to my back, then pushes me towards her.

When I reach the girl he says to her, 'Take it, put it in your mouth, and do not bite it off,' and I see him smirk, which makes him look very ugly.

She puts her lips around it first, licks it, then puts it right inside her mouth.

Kola then hitches up her skirt, pushes her to the ground and pulls off her knickers. 'Now get on top of her and put it in,' he says.

I lie on top of her, and he puts his boot on my buttocks, pushes me up and down. 'That's it,' he shouts, 'that's how you do it,' and laughs then, that hyena laugh.

I am not inside her, my thing is floppy, but he, Kola, cannot see this, at least I do not think he can.

I look at the girl's face now, she has her head tilted back, she looks very sad and afraid, and I worry that I am hurting her. I stop going up and down so hard.

'I've had enough of this,' Kola finally says, pulls me off of her, and orders Kisunga to do the same.

I watch while Kisunga fumbles awkwardly on top of her, until Kola becomes impatient, kicks him off of her, and pulls down his own trousers. 'I'll show you how it's done!' he shouts.

His thing is long and hard. He gets to his knees and forces himself onto her, she screams, he puts his hand over her mouth, then thrusts away, as if pounding a piece of meat, until she is silent.

He finally lets out a series of moans, his whole body tensing and straightening, as he thrusts once more and then is still, lying on top of her as if he has suddenly died.

'That's how you do it!' he then says coolly, getting to his feet and pulling up his trousers.

I look at the girl. She lies there, her skirt hitched up around her waist, her eyes wet with tears.

'Leave her,' he calls to me, slightly out of breath, 'and come here.'

I walk over to him.

'Now for the last test,' he says to me and Kisunga. 'You must fight each other.'

'No, I will not fight him. He is my friend,' I say firmly.

Kola goes to hit me, but before he can Captain steps in between us and says, 'That is why you must fight him.'

Me and Kisunga stand and face each other. We wear just our underpants. 'We have to do this,' Kisunga whispers.

'I will not,' I say, and Captain hits me then on the back of my head with his big hand.

I stumble and feel dizzy, then he grabs me by the neck, pulls me close to him, pushes his face right up against mine and grunts, 'If you do not, then I will kill him.'

'Kill me!' I shout. I am worried what I am becoming. I am worried what I will do to Kisunga if I fight him.

'You are brave,' Captain says, as he pulls out his handgun and puts it to Kisunga's head. 'As I said, I will kill him, not you.'

Kisunga hits me then, punches me hard on the nose. I know he does not want to do this, that he is trying to protect me, just as I am trying to protect him.

All the Seniors gather round us in a circle. I touch my nose, it feels like it might be broken. I look at my fingers, they are bloody. Kisunga stands over me, looking sad, as if inviting me to hit him now, and so I do, I punch him where he punched me.

I hear shouting, everyone is becoming excited.

Me and Kisunga exchange blows. He hits me, then I hit him. I start to feel more angry as we fight, not angry at him but at them, and myself.

The anger finally takes me over, and I stop punching and throw myself at Kisunga, grabbing him round the neck and pulling him to the ground. My arm around his neck, I feel a strong urge to really hurt him, squeeze his neck until he goes red in the face and starts making choking noises like a chicken that is having its neck wrung. I think about school, how we used to play fight – it seems like a long time ago. We would pretend to throw spears, swipe machetes and club one another with sticks, taking turns to attack and defend. I always enjoyed diving to the ground and rolling up into a ball when I had to defend myself. But this is not play now, no, this is real. I squeeze Kisunga's neck harder until he begins to choke, and when I loosen my grip briefly he spits and coughs, 'Stop! Stop!'

I let go of him, and get to my feet. Kisunga lies sprawled on the ground, clutching his throat. Captain walks over to me, hands me his gun and says, 'Finish him off.'

I am silent, just look at him with sadness in my eyes. He wants me to do to my friend Kisunga what he did to the small boy when we were first taken, shoot him dead in the head.

'Well?!' Captain shouts.

'Look, I have beaten him. Is that not enough?'

And Captain just chuckles, and says, 'I was only kidding. I do not want you to kill him. You both fought hard. Both of you shall become guerrillas now.'

∽

I have become one of them, it is no longer us and them. I am a Senior, and this brings more food and respect. They also give me an Aka. It looks old like the others, its metal is scratched and its wood is chipped, but it does not matter because it still fires. It is not a big gun like Kola's PK, that has three small legs mounted on its underside, forming a triangle, which means you can stand it on the ground, or on a rock or branch, and shoot from there. It also has many bullets that hang around Kola's neck like a giant necklace.

He, General Mushamuka, finally returns. It is late afternoon, the sun will be setting soon. We are all ordered to assemble in front of his home, a large red brick house. It must have at least four or five rooms. I have not seen a house like this in a long time. We are told he wants to address us.

I wonder what he will look like, this man who is meant to be 'everything that is wrong with the world'. I know his skin is light brown. I imagine he will be even bigger and fatter than the Commander, a giant man, and older too, maybe forty, and that he will have black eyes, blacker than the night. Perhaps he will not even appear as a man but rather a snake, a giant one like in my nightmare.

There must be three hundred of us standing here waiting for him. The Commander and Captain stand at the front, then the Seniors – I stand at the back of them as I am the youngest – and then the porters and girls. I catch sight of Okello and smile at him, which makes me less nervous.

He finally appears, and at first I am not sure it is him. He walks out of the door of his big house, I can barely see him, and steps up onto a small raised platform. I can see him better now. He is a small man, short and skinny, and older than I imagined him to be, about sixty. He wears white trousers and a white shirt. He does not look bad. To begin with he says nothing, just smiles at all of us assembled before him. Then he raises his arms in the air and everyone starts to shout and cheer. The setting sun behind him beams red, and standing there dressed all in white he almost looks like a God. Only when he puts his arms down is everyone silent again. There is a long wait before he at last speaks.

'One day we will be so strong that we will march on the capital, kill the President, and this great country will be ours once more. It has been taken away from us, and we must fight to get it back. Only then will this country be good, and its people be happy.

'The muzungu, arrogant and aloof, has made us weak. He judges us to be lazy and immoral, dirty and dumb.

He has destroyed village life, forcing us to abandon our homes and way of life in pursuit of precious minerals and resources, be these diamonds or oil. He has made us act solely in his service, for his benefit: we contribute to his economy and we collude with his greed.

'The white man might not rule any more, but he continues to dominate, be it through the imposition of trade barriers against our products, such as textiles and agricultural goods, the purchase of our vital resources, resources we can ill afford to give away, or the wooing of our best minds, the promise to these citizens of greater wealth and stability in Europe or the United States.

'We might have hailed our independence as the start of something wonderful, a renaissance in the country and across the continent, and yet we continue to struggle desperately: our people do nothing more than live, rather pathetically, on the remains of past colonial glory. And though it is far easier now for a black man to fuck a white woman this does little to redress the wrongs of the past.

'The muzungu remains willing to let our country, our whole continent, destroy itself. Billions of dollars of foreign aid has been sunk into Africa, but with little discernible result: we remain the world's poorest region. Even the condoms donated by international agencies end up on the black market and in the top drawers of corrupt government ministers' desks. For our President regards AIDS as a necessary evil to restrain population growth. Rather the people fuck, than shoot, themselves to death!

'He claims to respect us, his people, and yet he allows white men to have our women. He claims to protect us, his people, and yet he allows us to be beaten to death with hammers and iron bars in military bases and police stations. He claims to love us, his people, and yet he lets us starve, spending all his money on his precious golf course. This is a muzungu's game, and we do not want to play his, the white man's game, any more.

'Death to him, do you hear me?! Death to the muzungu! No more immunity for him. It is he that has brought us so much suffering, and all our President does is perpetuate this suffering. He claims that we are free from the white man now, but we are not. He still controls us, he still encourages the slave to kill the slave.

'Some of you ask why we kill our own if it is the muzungu who is responsible for all our misery? Well, this is because those of us who collude with the white man are as bad as he is, and they, these bilulu, like him, must be punished, stamped on. Let us cleanse our country! And we must be ruthless here, we must stop at nothing. So let us carry on burning their villages and taking their livestock and food. And let us take their children and make them our own!

'I will not rest until we are free of the muzungu and all his collaborators, these traitors, until this country is ours, is an African nation once more. We must hate and fight. God has given us this power. Hate and fight, hate and fight!'

There are great cheers at this moment as the General holds his arms in the air and waves to us all. Kola, who stands in front, turns round to look at me. I am not cheering and he is. He scowls at me, hisses, 'Cheer!'

And so I do, cheer like he does, even though I do not quite understand why I should be doing this. I am not sure of what the General says, about guerrillas ruling the country. He states that we guerrillas are good and that everyone who is against us is bad, but all we do is steal and loot and kill. How can that be good?

The celebration goes on well into the evening. Pombe is brought to us and we are told to drink and be merry. I have never had pombe, banana beer, before. It tastes bad and bitter, and I do not understand why grown-ups like it so much. But the more of it I drink, the more I like it. It makes my head feel light and dizzy, but also makes me happy and want to join in the dance. We start to sing songs about beating the President and making the country ours once more. There is suddenly so much hope all around me, and I feel it, it makes me feel good for the first time in ages, and I hope this feeling will not go away, will stay with me forever.

10

Pumbu, my half sister, is missing. I cannot see her.

Six and a half, and with a swollen perineum, she is very attractive to other males and has begun to flirt a little, with me in particular. She will be an adult soon. Were we bonobos we would no doubt already have engaged in some sexual activity: these primates possess a rampant enthusiasm for sex, uncannily close to humans in this respect, and yet far less inhibited.

Suddenly, I hear the sound of screaming – it is my aunt – as she also realises her daughter is missing.

She wakes my mother, who in turn wakes my father.

When he gets to his feet he immediately spots a human, a poacher, attempting to coax Pumbu away – I was sure that it was another silverback who could not resist a young female in oestrus – and with this he roars, the whole forest woken abruptly from its dreams… turacos, coucals, warblers, scorpions, toads, chameleons, bushbucks, duikers, civets, golden cats, giant forest hogs, all these species and more, disturbed by the screams of my father as he charges off in the direction of his young daughter. I was right to worry, after all.

I watch the intruder stand his ground at first – he has two dogs and carries a spear. It looks like he might challenge my father, but he backs off as my father gets closer and he is forced to take in his sheer size.

My father belch-grunts, calling Pumbu to him as the poacher flees, then returns her to the arms of my aunt.

I take this opportunity to challenge him about his view of humans – I want my father to consider whether they are, perhaps, ultimately bad, not good – but he is in no mood for this, and with furrowed brow pig-grunts harshly, warning me off. I immediately step back into the clutches of the Dombeya rotundifolia behind me and lower my head, feeling guilty now. Though my mother perceives my sceptical nature as symptomatic of my age – I am still a teenager, after all – my father is not quite so accommodating: he will always challenge my negativity, whatever age I am. And he remains adamant that he is better placed to judge humans than I am: for he has experienced, and observed, more of them – he simply knows them better than I do.

But humans, it seems to me, do struggle to appreciate quite how loving, nurturing and protective we gorillas are with our young: we will do anything for them. And this devotion is not only to our young. I remember at this moment, as I watch Pumbu nestle in my aunt's arms, how distraught my father was when my grandmother was dying. I was just seven. He sat by her the last three days of her life – she was suffering from pneumonia and pleurisy – gently grooming and caressing her – her balding head, her wrinkled face, her greying muzzle – which he did almost obsessively, so determined was he to comfort her. He actually left the group, such was his maternal devotion. He wanted, and needed, to be with her when she died. It was as if he was, quite simply, unwilling to let his own mother suffer the fate of so many other old mothers, left to die alone in the hollow bowls of trees. And when she finally did die, he spent hours nudging her body and slapping her face, desperate to draw a response from her…a furrowed brow, a pig-grunt, anything.

I look away from Pumbu now, and over at him, my father. Where will he take us? I wonder.

11

When I wake up the next morning my head aches. It must be because of all the pombe I drank. Captain marches towards us. 'A lookout has just seen government soldiers nearby, about twenty of them,' he says. 'We're going to attack them before they attack us.'

The Commander appears. 'I want forty of you, now!' he shouts.

Kola walks up behind me and whispers in my ear, 'You have a chance to get your gumboots, little Kibwe. Are you up to it, can you kill a man?' he goads me.

I turn round and look at him with a hard face, as if I am able to, able to kill someone, even though I do not think I am. I hear my mother's voice in my ear, about never doing bad, and think of the Ten Commandments.

'Let us go!' Captain shouts, and orders us to pick up our guns and follow him and the Commander.

We creep slowly through the bush towards the main road, where we see two lorries pulled up. Both of them are open-topped. Some government soldiers sit inside, others stand around outside. Captain whispers, 'Stop,' then tells us to split up into ten groups of four. 'We will ambush them.'

We quickly divide into groups. 'We will form a circle around the two trucks until we have them surrounded,' he continues. 'Only fire when I give the order.' And with these words all the groups head off in different directions.

Me and Kisunga follow Kola and one other Senior whose name I do not know. When we reach the side of the road, about two hundred yards up from the lorries, we wait in a ditch until we are sure that none of the government soldiers are looking, then scamper across the road like cunning jackals. I am the last to cross, and as I do I hear a shhh…shhh…shhh, these noises whizzing over my head, and then realise that these are shots being fired. They must have seen us.

Suddenly there is an explosion of noise, bullets flying in every direction. I dive behind a matoke tree on the other side of the road and stand rigid, like a scared bushbuck, behind its trunk. I peer round and see two government soldiers running towards me, then look back, my eyes darting wildly around, in search of the others. Where have they gone?

Staring ahead again I see that one of the government soldiers is close now, the muzzle of his gun flashing in the bright light of the early morning sun. I stand out from behind the tree, holding my gun, about to point it in his direction, but then I freeze, unable to point the barrel at him, let alone pull the trigger.

When he sees me like this he does not shoot right away. He is a man, not a boy like me. He shouts, 'Put your gun down!' This scares me, and when I do not he just fires, shoots me in the ribs, and I cry out in pain.

I drag myself behind the tree, crawling on my hands and knees like a wounded animal, clutching my side, then pull up my T-shirt and see a big red hole in my ribs. I remember what Captain said to us when we were training, that if we are shot we must put our fingers in the wound and get the bullet out. I manage to do this and lots of blood comes out, it is a deep hole, so I take off my T-shirt and tie it around my ribs to try and stop it bleeding any more. I do not want to lose all my blood, because if I do then I will die.

I sense that the government soldier who shot me is right behind the tree. He cannot see me, but knows I am wounded. Play dead, I suddenly think, more of Captain's words in training coming to me, and so I slump down against the trunk and close my eyes, still holding my Aka though, but to the ground so it looks like I have just let it go.

Keeping my eyes closed, I listen carefully for his footsteps as he walks around the tree to face me. He is standing over me now, he must think I am dead. I wait…until I hear him rest what I think is the butt of his gun on the ground, then open my eyes very quickly, lift my Aka and fire, guh-guh-guh.

I have shot him, I realise, as I watch him drop his gun, clasp his neck with both hands and fall to the ground. He calls out for his friend, shouting, 'Help!', making a gurgling noise, which must be all the blood in his throat making him choke, and next is just silent…

His arms flop either side of his body, like two dead fish on hooks, and then his breathing stops, his stomach no longer going up and down.

I remember now what the Commander said to us when we first kill someone. We should put our 'finger on the blood of the dead person, and then lick it', because if we do this then we will not have bad dreams after. But I do not want to do this. He also told us we should 'enjoy the mastery, the power of killing, of taking another man's life'. But it is wrong to enjoy this, it cannot be right, and I do not feel excited about what I have done, just scared and bad. Kola told me that General Mushamuka 'eats the livers of the men he kills', and I thought he was lying. Maybe he was not.

The other government soldier appears, he is a grown-up as well. He shoots his gun and the bullet skims my head, clipping the hair and scalp. This makes my head hurt, but I try my level best to lift up my Aka, turn towards him and shoot. I hit him in his stomach and he falls down onto his back. I hear him breathing very deeply as blood pours out of his tummy.

I lie there covered in blood, coughing and hawking and spitting, blood coming from my mouth, and wonder now why I did not just let them kill me, because at least then my suffering would have stopped, I would no longer be a guerrilla, have to walk all day, raid camps, and do bad things, kill people.

It seems I am lying here for a long time, I do not know how long, before the Commander comes with three other Seniors. All the shooting has finally stopped. 'We killed them all!' the Commander says.

The government soldier I shot in the stomach is still alive. The Commander walks over to him. 'He's ugly, looks like a gorilla,' he grunts, then bends down and puts his ear to his chest. 'Still breathing,' he says, looking up at me and smiling.

The Commander then slowly pulls his machete out of his belt and draws it across the soldier's neck, his head falling back as if it might just drop off like a chicken's, blood pouring from it. 'Not any more!' he finishes off.

He does not taste his blood, and I think this must be because he has killed so many people that he does not need to any more.

'You have done well,' he says to me. 'Now you have your gumboots,' and he pulls them off the first government soldier I shot and throws them to me. 'Get two porters to take him back to the sick bay,' he says to the Seniors, then walks away.

I am carried back to headquarters and into the sick bay, just a large tent with lots of mats on the floor. It is mainly for women and girls who are sick or pregnant. The wound in my ribs smells bad already, like a rotten vegetable, lots of pus there.

On the first morning one of the porters comes with a washbowl of hot water. It is Ojok, and I am very happy to see him. He says, 'Kibwe, they have told me I must show you how to clean your wound. This will help you get better.'

'Okay,' I reply.

Ojok pours the hot water onto the wound, then washes away the pus with a small towel and lays some blackjack on top of it. 'I'll leave this towel with you and bring you hot water as often as I can.'

He holds my hand at this moment, clutches it tight, and this makes me think of my mother, how she used to hold my hand and squeeze it to show how much she loved me. Before he goes, he fills a flask with cold water and tells me to drink as much as I can.

I grab the flask, drink from it, then pour some water into my hand, which I splash onto my face. I do this again, and again, it feels nice. As I lean over and go to do it one last time I see my face in the water and blink, am startled, because I look different, there is a mad look in my eye, and I wonder if this will always be there from now on, now that I have killed one man and shot another.

I am in the sick bay for two weeks, though it seems much longer because I have nothing to do but just lie there on the ground. Every day a woman comes – she is the nurse I think – and gives me some pills to take. I do not know what they are. They tell me that a witch-doctor will come, but he does not.

I like the nights, as I can just lie there and stare through the hole in the side of the tent up at the stars. I join them up, making lots of different shapes. But I do not like it when I finally fall asleep, because it is then that that the cockroaches come out and clamber all over my sick and smelly body. Their favourite part is the large scab which is forming on my ribs – it is a bit like the back of a big black beetle. It is also then that I dream about the men that I shot, and this makes me think that maybe I should have done what the Commander said and tasted the blood. Sometimes my dreams about them are so bad that I cry, but I must do this silently because I am worried what the others will think if they hear me. I find myself waking every hour, the salty taste of tears in my mouth, shaking, sweating, the faces of the dead men smiling at me through bloody mouths and faces, the air thick with the smell of their dead bodies, which makes me retch. God, oh no, what have I done?! He is punishing me now.

Tonight is horrible. I lie alone and feel strange, like I am outside myself, watching myself, and I do not like what I see. I see someone who has done a very bad thing. Maybe it is the men I shot, who are now ghosts, getting their revenge, trying to drive me crazy. I start to laugh, laughing alone in the dark, and then cry. If my mother knew what I did to these two men she would never talk to me again, she would stop loving me, I am sure. What can I do? I ask myself.

The Commander comes to see me the next morning and says, 'When you are out of the sick bay I want you to be one of my escorts.' He does not call me by my name, maybe he still does not know it. This means that I must guard him, follow him wherever he goes, and make sure he is not hurt.

I reply quietly, 'Yes, Commander.'

'What are you thinking about?' he asks me. I know I cannot tell him about my nightmares, that I feel bad about killing, so I just say, 'I am thinking about my mother and am sad because I am not with her.'

'You have a new family now,' he says, then leaves me.

12

This evening, at sunset, I climb a tree in order to obtain a view of the sky – it is practically impossible to see it from the forest floor – and it is stunning, crimson-coloured, its gentle, diminishing light touching everything. Africa, this great, diverse continent of wilderness and free-living animals, I feel such freedom under its vast skies, as I do in its forests, these splendid kingdoms of silence, which I love to walk in, along lengthy meadow corridors, these natural pathways carpeted with a range of grasses, clovers and wild flowers.

And yet death is always close at hand – every living thing is perpetually reminded of its mortality – though it is this facet which makes this continent the very heart of the world. It might at times be hard and brutal, but this does not mean its character is ugly. Far from it, it is quite beautiful.

I look down at my mother as she goes to sit, but then she screams, a high-pitched noise, and I know immediately that something is seriously wrong.

I climb down from the tree and join my father, who has run to her aid. She carries a wire noose around her ankle. My father attempts to pull it off with his teeth. He repeatedly grunts with frustration. He tries for a number of hours, but in vain.

He is furious, with himself as well as with the human who laid the snare. Perhaps the poacher, who he saw off just weeks prior to this, is responsible. He should have moved us right after the last incursion. He expresses more anger now than I have seen before. He might have always tried to be hopeful about humans – confident that they might, ultimately, become less aggressive, less domineering, that their goodness might prevail – but now it is as if he has all but given up on them...has finally renounced his optimism, just like that. In truth, his rage at this moment frightens me.

When night comes and we sleep, my mother quietly moans – the metal is sinking into her ankle, it is no doubt becoming infected.

The next morning my father tries again, but still cannot get it off. I try as well, but to no avail. We must keep moving: he has finally decided to move us to another area, off the gentle lower slopes and higher up.

We walk for a long time, far more than the usual kilometre per day, and my mother soon becomes dehydrated and a little emaciated, her whole body humped and angular.

After almost a week my father finally manages to get the wire off of her – had he not she might have lost her whole leg to gangrene – using his canines to slide the wire free.

Thankfully she is able to clean the wound orally. Had it been on her head or back she might have died from the infection.

She retches a lot for a number of days and her body exudes a sour odour. My father has to make sure the rest of the group travels more slowly in order to accommodate her and assist her recuperation.

It takes my mother a fair amount of time to return to full strength, to overcome the dehydration, shock and septicaemia. Were my father less devoted he might well have simply let her die. The majority of gorilla groups cannot afford to have one member who prevents them from moving when they need to, and my father has to work especially hard to appease my increasingly restless and poorly behaved half brothers, juveniles who have had enough of the slow pace.

Humans fear the other animals who still live freely here, and yet they need not, my father insists, finally calmer now. It is only ignorance or folly which will endanger them, and yet increasingly, they either hunt and kill these other species or confine them to national parks and reserves, unwilling to grant them the freedom that they, humans, possess. Sadly, they seem increasingly to view all other life as an obstacle, that is unless it is economically valuable.

The only predator we gorillas now face is Homo sapiens. In light of all this species' hunting, the leopards have all but gone. My father recalls their numbers when he was my age – there were many. When he was an infant these big cats used to prey on him and his siblings – try and snatch them during the night from the arms of my grandparents while they slept – but they were driven away by humans' traps, snares and guns, which at one stage were everywhere as rival poachers competed for the next big kill. And so now, just a few leopards remain, and we gorillas are the kings of the forest. Yes, there are forest elephant, buffalo and antelope, big mammals also, which we still share the land with, but they pose no threat to us and so we let them be. If only humans could follow our example, I muse. They have killed these animals in their millions. Why must they compete against, and dominate, every species they encounter?

At this moment I go to scoop some soil from beneath me, only to see a handful of swallow's eggs. I promptly move away: I do not want to disturb these young.

13

I do not like being the Commander's escort. He tells me that I am to be his protector until the day I die, which means for the rest of my life. But I do not want to protect him. I worry that if I am close to him for too long then I might become like him. He says he believes in God, that he is doing God's work, but I want to say to him, 'If you believe in God, then why do you kill so many innocent people?' Yet I know that he would get very angry if I said this, so angry that his eyes would go funny and he might just kill me, like all the others. So I am silent.

My first mission with him is to a boarding school. It is a two-day march, and we must cross a river. At least I have gumboots now. 'The General wants more recruits!' he declares as we march off into the bush.

We make the journey in a day and a half, then wait till it is night before we enter the school. When we get near to the main gate, Captain orders two Seniors to go ahead and pretend to be government soldiers. They approach the guard on the gate, and before he is given time to realise they are guerrillas one of them grabs him by the arms while the other slashes his throat.

Captain and his regiment break into the boys' dormitory, while the Commander and his break into the girls'.

Some of the boys from their dormitory manage to escape and run towards the girls' dormitory in a bid to protect them. Kola turns on them with his PK and shoots two of them dead. The other few run away.

On the way out we raid the dispensary, stealing lots of sweets and sodas. We are so hungry that we gorge on them and then feel sick.

We leave the school with twelve boys and fifteen girls. One girl refuses to be tied up, and so the Commander beats her with the handle of his panga until she is dead. He walks past me when he has finished, snorting and spitting, and his eyes are blank, like there is nothing behind them. They all start to cry when they see him do this, all the boys and girls, and he shouts, 'If any of you continue to cry then I will kill you like I just killed her. I will beat you to death!' And this immediately reminds me of what Captain said when he abducted me and the others, and this makes me shudder. It seems like such a long time ago that we were taken.

The Commander orders us to start walking. He is sure that government soldiers nearby must have heard gunshots. 'Keep a close eye on them,' he says to me, pointing at the boys and girls we have taken.

We walk for four hours until the sun is beginning to rise, then stop. I watch Wasswa slaughter one goat and Kola another, goats we stole from the school, slitting their throats, hacking off their limbs, and cutting up their bodies into small pieces. They bring the meat over to the girls and tell them to cook it. At first they do not want to, because they think it is either lizard or snake. This is what they think guerrillas eat. I used to think the same thing. But Wasswa tells them they must, otherwise there will be trouble. He also assures them that it is goat, and that they should eat some of it as well, as they will need the strength for the long journey ahead.

It is very good to eat fatty and greasy meat after two days of just sorghum. We eat it all, all of us are so hungry, even the brains and the tongue, and I gnaw on a hoof when most of us have finished eating, because my stomach is still not full.

The Commander does not like one of the girls, I do not quite know why. She is older than the rest, about seventeen, skinny, with knobbly knees, and she has very short hair. Right away he starts to pick on her. 'Why do you look at me this way, you silly girl?!' he says to her in his deep grumbling voice. 'You are ugly, you look like a boy, has anyone ever told you that? No worse, an ape!'

I wish he would not be so cruel to her, but I dare not say anything to him.

'What do your parents do, girl?' he asks her.

She does not reply at first.

'Are you deaf?!' he goes on.

'You must answer him,' I whisper, nudging her arm.

She mumbles, 'My father is dead and my mother is a nurse.'

'Speak up, girl!'

'My father...'

'I heard you the first time,' he bellows. 'My mother was a nurse as well. She looked just like you. But she was no mother to me!' he says angrily.

The girl says nothing, just stares at his big belly.

'What the fuck are you looking at?!' he goes on, and we all know what she is looking at.

She does not answer, because she knows that if she does he will get even angrier with her.

He changes the subject. 'What do you want to do when you leave school?'

'I want to be a doctor,' she replies.

'What, so you can just look after government soldiers like your mother does, after I have beaten them half to death, these weak men who dare not be guerrillas?'

'I would look after everyone,' she says.

'I bet your mother just looks after government soldiers,' and with these words he smacks her across the back of the head with his massive hand and she falls, like a rag doll, face-down on the ground.

I let her take my arm as she pulls herself to her feet. I look into her eyes, and it is as if she has suddenly lost all hope.

'You must keep walking,' I say to her as the Commander walks ahead.

I find out her name. She is called Lydia. It gets hotter throughout the day, the sky more pink, the bush scrubbier. The heat haze makes it almost impossible to see. My eyes feel dry in their sockets. It is like the sun is cooking us. We finally come to the river in the late afternoon. We are nearly halfway back to headquarters. Few of us can swim, though I can, my father taught me. As before, two Seniors jump in. One of them ties the rope to a tree trunk on our side of the bank, while the other swims, with the other end of the rope, to a tree on the other side and ties it there.

Though many of the girls are unable to swim, they can use the rope to get across, can just pull themselves along. But Lydia is scared and a very bad swimmer. She gets in, but is not strong enough. She ate very little of the goat this morning, she is weak with hunger. She all of a sudden lets go and starts to panic, her arms flailing in the water like the wings of a fly that has fallen on its back in a puddle. I immediately dive in and swim over to her, put her arm over my shoulder, then take her safely to the other side.

But the Commander is furious with me for doing this and starts shouting, his mouth right in my face, spit coming from it and white froth gathering at its sides like he is boiling inside. 'Why did you do this for her? Who takes care of you, feeds you, protects you? I do! Is it because you want to fuck her?! You should have simply let her die. When we get back to headquarters you will be punished.' He then grabs Lydia by the arm and says, 'Let us set up camp here for the night,' then takes her off into thick bush. I know what he is going to do to her, and a few minutes later I hear her cries.

I do not sleep well that night, because I keep on thinking about Lydia and how I will be punished. They have taken my gun away from me.

In the morning I hear Kola shouting at all the girls, 'Line up, line up. Commander Kalango and Captain Djeke want to see you. And take off your clothes, all of them.'

We watch as the girls shyly remove their night-dresses, which they still wear since their abduction.

'And your underwear!' Kola shouts excitedly.

They nervously remove their pants and bras.

'You must choose husbands. Commander Kalango and Captain Djeke are coming now,' Kola continues.

'How can we choose husbands when we are so young, and when we do not even know the men you are telling us to marry?' one of the girls asks.

'Well, that bitch over there knows Commander Kalango well enough already,' he hisses, pointing hatefully at Lydia. 'And if you refuse to choose, then I will put this burning hot panga on your backs,' he says, removing it from the small fire next to him and holding it up so all the girls can see. Its big blade glows orange and red. 'They are like big silverback gorillas. They take as many females as they want!'

I watch as they make their choices. Lydia chooses the Commander, even after what he did to her yesterday.

∽

When we finally get back to headquarters, the Commander orders Kola to take me to solitary. This is a small wooden cage built of bamboo. I am locked inside it, I am terrified. There are three of these cages, and two small boys occupy the other two. They are younger than me, maybe eight or nine, and look very weak. It is the middle of the day and there is no shade. We are guarded by two Seniors with PKs.

I am left there for two days with no food or water. My tongue starts to feel very heavy, like it has a big stone on it and I cannot lift it up. I drink some of my urine, but it tastes dirty and salty. I have not suffered like this since I was first abducted.

I start to dig in the ground, desperate to try and get water, but I cannot find any. All I find is some damp soil. I lie down on my back and put it on my chest and stomach and legs. It is cooling. But still I feel my body drying up, all the water leaving it.

The third morning I awake I realise that the two boys in the cages beside me are dead. They must have died during the night. Flies and midges buzz around their bodies. This is it, I will die like them, I think.

But I do not feel scared any more. The fear has gone. Instead I feel quite peaceful, because I think it might finally stop...all this. When you suffer a lot, when you live against how you want to live, then anything that happens happens...is in God's hands. A few other boys have shot themselves, but not me. And anyway, I do not want to guard the Commander any more because he is a bad man. He has raped many girls and he likes to kill. I remember now how Kola bragged one night that 'the Commander is so ruthless that he once necklaced a man'. I did not know what he meant by this until Wasswa told me. He poured petrol into a tyre, slung it around a man's neck, and then set light to it. Kola said he watched the man burn alive, 'his eyes popping like boiled eggs'. The Commander's blood is going to go to his head one day, God is going to judge him...I know this.

The Commander finally comes to me. He walks fast, holding his handgun not his panga, and I am sure that he is just going to pull me out of the cage and shoot me dead. But the first thing he does is order away the two Seniors guarding me. He waits then...waits until they are some way off...saying nothing. He then unlocks the cage and says, 'Get out, get down on your knees.'

I do this, and hold my head down, waiting for him to kill me. I feel the cold metal of his gun on my forehead. He is breathing heavily, fffuuuhhh...fffuuuhhh, and I look up at him, his massive white teeth clenched together and spit coming through the gap in his front teeth.

'Do not look at me!' he shouts, breathing even faster.

And so I close my eyes and just wait…

'I cannot do it, I cannot do it…' he finally mumbles and I feel the gun slide off my head and watch his arm fall to his side.

He then throws his arms around me and just holds me and kisses my head, muttering my name for the first time, and saying, 'Kibwe, do not disobey me again.'

I did not think he could ever be kind like this, but just bad and cruel. Before I was a guerrilla, if I had come this close to death but had survived, then I would have cried. But now I have no tears in my eyes…they are empty like buckets with no water left in them. I have to make myself feel nothing in order to carry on.

I hear shots then, and know that we are under attack from government soldiers. The Commander lets go of me, and as he does so a grenade lands just a few feet from us, and we must dive for cover.

'Those motherfuckers!' the Commander screams as he lands hard on the ground, 'I'm going to hack them to pieces!'

His eyes flash wild as he gets to his feet and pulls out his panga from his belt.

We both go to run, but as we do a mortar bomb hurtles towards us, slamming into a tree right beside us, and we are thrown backwards by the blast.

Everything is still for a moment, smoke thick in the air, I cannot see anything. My right leg tingles,

I look down at it, it is bloody. I cannot see the Commander…

I get up and run, even though my leg is hurting a lot, just run and run, my heart beating so fast I feel like my chest is on fire. My whole body trembles with the thought that I might be free. I run until I cannot lift my leg any more, until it just quivers beneath me, feeling light and floppy, unable to support the weight of my upper body.

I find a big tree and lie down against its trunk. I know I must give my leg time to rest. I lean over and start grabbing at leaves and other brushwood on the floor. I must try and camouflage myself. My heart continues to pound, and I say a prayer, 'God, please protect me.'

part **2**

14

It is clear we are ever more at risk now, even though we have moved to another part of the forest: we are higher up than we were before; giant heath is prevalent here. There seem to be a greater number of traps and snares; there seems to be increased fighting between the government and the guerrillas.

It is just gone midday, and my father and I stand on the edge of our new territory and look down the slopes towards the human habitat below. We can no longer escape them, it seems, wherever we run to – cultivated land in the foreground and a small town in the background, the latter growing day by day, getting closer and closer to the forest, to our home. When will they stop encroaching on us?

The sky is blue, we have a clear view, there is not a cloud in sight. I sense that the humans are becoming increasingly desperate, and during such times I know will resort to anything in order to survive: it is difficult for them to be good when they are hungry and unhappy.

My father and I observe, first, a small church, which has been erected on the edge of the town, and see a black priest standing outside it seeing off his congregation. He is no doubt more conservative and orthodox than his European counterparts. The many Christian missionaries here are still convinced that their religion is the only route to salvation for the African people, and it is their level of conviction which makes them quite so dangerous. The policy of divide and rule worked well for the European imperialists, Christianity offered as the one unifying force to end all tribal conflict. And yet many Africans have adopted the white man's faith and a few have used it to perpetrate evil rather than good.

My father believes that the war which rages here, which threatens us and other animals, is driven by religion, which humans have a great predilection for. They like to engage in it – in rituals and prayer and belief – it helping them to live in a world not as kind to them as they might hope. But it also acts as a form of social control, in a positive sense providing coherence and a sense of control over the uncertainties of life, but in a negative sense imposing often constrictive rules of behaviour in human society and permitting a minority to wield power. The world is a tough place to survive in – we gorillas know this all too well – and seems to continually present its inhabitants with situations beyond their control. Humans require something which will protect and soothe them, in which they will find solace. The common theme of every religion is that its members are the elect, chosen by God, and such a belief, a kind of divine guarantee, provides a profound sense of comfort in the face of adversity.

In light of the above it is no wonder why religion has such a stranglehold over humans, why they so readily succumb to the demands of religious zealots in spite of their intellect. I think that my love for my mother and father provides me with a feeling akin to religious experience. Perhaps my parents have become my religion. In which case, religion is not the sole domain of humans, who would do well to remember that their hominid ancestors, the Cro-Magnons, only discovered it about five hundred thousand years ago.

If I stare hard enough at this moment, in the bright light of the early afternoon, I can see beyond the church to the soldiers in the centre of the town patrolling the streets, armed with white world hand-me-downs, cold-war-era weaponry, Kalashnikovs slung carelessly over their shoulders like they are clothing accessories rather than instruments of death. My father has heard these guns, and run from them, his whole life. We gorillas can no longer avoid humans' countless tools, be these traps, guns or motor vehicles: they have become sadly familiar. The guerrilla leader Mushamuka is convinced that he is more virtuous, more God-fearing than the incumbent president, and consequently the people will fare better under him, under more righteous leadership, not least because they will no longer be forced to submit to the will of the white man, which they have done for far too long. Humans like to differentiate between themselves as well as between the various primate species. In fact, they seek distinction everywhere, obsessed with their own uniqueness. And so one tribe is greater than another, one colour of people superior to another. It goes on and on.

Alongside these soldiers my father points out the NGO workers, grunting and gesticulating with his head, and I see them now, as I sit down, parading down the dusty gravel road in their brand new white 4x4s – adorned with flags and logos, these great symbols of the civilised, benign world of the US and Europe – protected by armed guards. The local children might not be safe, but the white aid workers are.

Though my father and I have a different idea of poverty, the human poverty before us now is clear enough: there are few brick buildings, few goods for sale other than the bare essentials. The only indication of the modern is the presence of a glossy Western-owned petrol station, which stands awkwardly on the edge of the town and provides fuel that is desperately over-priced, and which only the white NGOs can afford. It is no wonder the local economy struggles to develop: small businesses simply cannot afford to transport their goods. And in the fields just below us we can see men dressed in yellow jumpsuits working the land: they make prisoners work out their time here.

I suggest to my father, as we continue to watch this scene below, which is given clarity by the dazzling blue of the sky, that we should move again, that they, the humans, are still too close, but he is adamant that we stay now, that we do not run any more. He holds his head in his hands and rubs his forehead, wearily. If it is not poachers who will get to us, then it will be the guerrillas – they will kill us for sport, I maintain. But my father shushes me, grunting softly. He insists that it will not be long before humans look into our eyes and finally see what we see in one another, a clear sense of the past and future. Their long-held belief that we possess no sense of either is untrue. In fact, when they do at last see this, grasp this reality, they will see and grasp other things also, he maintains, behaviours and tendencies remarkably similar to their own. The one shared trait, which immediately comes to mind, is curiosity: like humans, we gorillas are interested in practically everything, and right now my father and I cannot stop watching all that is going on below us, the relentless march of human activity.

We often laugh amongst ourselves about how they perceive us. Most amusing of all is their conviction that we all look the same and do not possess individual characters. They fail to realise, first, that though they might struggle to tell us apart from one another, we have no such difficulty. Just like humans, gorillas come in many different shapes and sizes: some possess beauty, others strength, and others something else entirely. We are distinguishable by our noseprints, not our fingerprints, and by the shapes of our nostrils and outstanding troughs on the bridge of our noses. We are as sensitive to these facial differences as humans are to theirs. And second, just like them, we possess unique characters, vivid personalities: some of us are even-tempered and patient, others volatile and rash; some are thoughtful and compassionate, others inconsiderate and cruel.

My father finally turns to leave as the sun begins to set – we have been here all afternoon – and though he has decided that we will remain where we are, and not go deeper into the forest, from here on he wants Kibu and me to take up sentry positions as a matter of course.

I continue to stare down at the town below, my arms crossed anxiously over my chest, until my father belch-grunts, urging me to get to my feet and follow him. For it will be dark soon.

15

When I wake up I have no idea where I am. I am very thirsty, my throat feels raw and cracked, there is no spit in my mouth. It is early morning. How far am I from the headquarters? I do not know. But I do know this is my chance to escape. Me, Kisunga, Ojok and Okello used to say to each other that if we managed to escape then this meant God loved us. I say prayers, then I move once more. My leg hurts a lot, but I try not to think about it. I make myself run through the pain.

At last I reach a road. It is deserted. I walk for a kilometre or so until I come to a mango tree. I pick one of its fruits, tear the skin off with my front teeth, spit this out, then take a big bite, savouring the juicy orange flesh as I chew on it and swallow it fast. I am starving. It also helps quench my thirst.

I think of my family, my mother and father, and my friends, and I hold pictures of all their faces in my mind. Whenever they came to mind before I did not do this, picture their faces, because this just made me sad, but now I feel that I can, because I have escaped, I am free from the guerrillas.

Sitting down against the mango tree, I look down at my body. It is dirty and bloody. I reach over and grab a clump of grass, drawing its morning dew into my hands, then wiping this over my arms and legs, trying to clean myself, at least get rid of some of the blood. But I need more water than this, I know, I need it to rain, and just as I think this it starts to, lightly at first, then heavily. I remove all my clothes, even my underpants, and then just stand there naked in it as it pours down, my head tilted up to the sky, mouth open, as I drink it in, then use it to clean my body.

Suddenly I hear voices, and look round to see four government soldiers staring at me, smiling, their guns pointed towards me. 'Hold your hands up,' the youngest of them says. He looks like he is about eighteen.

Standing there naked in the rain, I do this, and then begin to cry, cry so much that I cannot stop. I just sob and sob.

'Why are you crying?' he finally asks.

'It is okay, child,' the oldest one says. He is about the same age as Commander Kalango. 'Pick up your clothes and come with us.'

∽

We walk down the road towards a jeep. I am limping badly now. When we reach it, the driver throws me a towel and says, pointing to the back of the vehicle, which is shielded from the rain by a green canvas roof, 'Get in, dry yourself down and put on your clothes.'

The oldest one offers me some water and a biscuit, then says, 'Do you know where they have fled to?'

'No, when you attacked I just ran.'

'You are not lying to us, are you?!' the youngest one butts in.

'No,' I answer.

'Take him back to the barracks,' the oldest one says to the driver, and one of you go in the back with him.

I sit in the jeep as we drive down lots of small bush tracks before we come to the barracks and park outside two big brick buildings. One is the Command Centre, this written in red paint on the front door, and the other, I am not sure. Perhaps it is where one of the government's generals or commanders lives. At the back of these buildings are a host of mud and tin huts, the soldiers' quarters, where they live with their families. Young half-naked children potter about between different huts, while women sit outside their homes, either washing clothes or cooking.

The soldier guarding me in the back of the jeep says, 'Get out.'

I see a number of soldiers lounging in the shade under a grass-roofed shelter. Everything they wear is green – the short-sleeved shirt, the trousers, the gum-boots. Their guns, all Akas, lie beside them.

He takes me into the Command Centre, then into a small office, and tells me to sit down in front of a big desk. He calls to a woman in the kitchen, who I can see through the door, to bring me some food, maize porridge, two cups of it. She hands me a small bowl of sugar as well, she has a kind face, and I pour it into both cups. It is a little lumpy, but tastes so sweet, like the best meal in the world. While I am eating another man enters. He looks important, he has a small moustache, and he sits down behind the big desk. He watches me as I eat. He waits until I have finished before he says anything.

'I am Captain Talian, and I need to ask you some questions,' and with these words he picks up the pen on his desk and opens the notepad to a blank page.

'Okay,' I mumble as I swallow the last mouthful of porridge.

'What is your name?'

'Kibwe.'

'Kibwe what?'

'Kibwe Charles.' I watch him write my name down.

'How old are you?'

'Eleven.'

'How long were you with them for?'

'I was abducted last September.'

'Almost a year, then.'

'Yes, I suppose so,' I reply, realising that my life in the bush as a guerrilla has made me lose all sense of time.

'Were you a guerrilla, or just a porter?'

'I…'

'If you were a guerrilla, it is okay, just tell me.'

'Yes, I was.'

'A guerrilla?'

'Yes.'

'Where is your gun, then? My men say that you had no gun on you when they found you.'

'They took it off me when they put me in solitary.'

'Why did they put you in solitary?'

'I helped a girl I was not meant to help.'

'Right…and did you kill any government soldiers while you were a guerrilla?'

I do not want to say that I did. This might make him cross, and he might just kill me in his office.

'Kibwe, did you?'

'Yes,' I say quietly.

'How many?'

'I killed one and shot another.'

'Was this when we attacked the headquarters?'

'No, it was before.'

'When?'

'About a month earlier, I think, but I am not sure.'

'Do you know what happened to the second man you shot?'

'He died.'

'So you killed two men, then.'

'No, the Commander killed him. He killed him with his machete.'

'Which Commander?'

'Commander Kalango.'

'Right,' and when I say his name Captain Talian nods like he has heard his name many times before, and writes again. I cannot read what he is writing.

'So you were at the guerrilla headquarters when we attacked?'

'Yes, in solitary.'

'Was General Mushamuka there?'

'Yes, I think so.'

'And Commander Kalango?'

'Yes, he was there. I was with him when you attacked.'

'But you said you were in solitary?'

'I was. He came to me there, I thought he was going to kill me, but he did not,' and then I find myself staring at the electric bulb above me, which casts its light over the dirty, blood-stained grey concrete walls of the office.

'D'you know where they are now, General Mushamuka and Commander Kalango?'

'No.'

'You are telling me the truth, Kibwe?'

'Yes, I am. I do not know. When you fired a mortar at us I lost the Commander, and then just ran.'

'Okay.'

There is a knock at the door at this moment, and a woman is brought in. I recognise her. She is about twenty and has a big belly, she must be pregnant. 'We found her just outside the barracks,' the soldier says. 'She says she escaped. She says she was one of Kalango's wives.'

Seeing her makes me think of Lydia. I wonder what has happened to her.

'Please, sit down over there,' Captain Talian says to her. 'I just need to finish talking to Kibwe. Do you know each other?'

'No, but I do recognise your face from the headquarters,' I say to her.

'And do you recognise Kibwe?' he asks her.

'Yes, I do,' she replies.

'Would you like to go back in the bush?' Captain Talian asks me.

'No.'

'Why not?'

'Because being a guerrilla is bad, and I never wanted to do the things they made me do.'

'What do you want to do now?'

'I want to go back home, I want to see my mother and father, I want to see my friends.'

'Okay,' Captain Talian says, finally speaking softly and smiling at me for the first time.

16

I am frustrated with Kibu. We are sentries now, we have a responsibility to ensure the welfare of the group, and he is not stationed where he should be, on the periphery of our territory. He knows we are under greater threat, thus must appreciate how important it is that we obey our father's instructions. But no, he has chosen not to stand guard any more, perhaps he is simply bored, and has made his way down the main slope to Pumbu, whom he pig-grunts at as she settles down to doze in her well-made nest – he wants her to vacate it so he can have it for himself. I feel a surge of anger course through me, and before I know it I am grunting and lunging at him. I not only hate it when he neglects his duties, but also when he acts like a bully and victimises weaker members of the group. He must be shown that such behaviour will not be tolerated. If our father will not discipline him, then I will. I mock-bite him and pig-grunt loudly, making it clear to Kibu, first, that he is putting all of us in jeopardy, and second, that though he might still be a blackback, he just has to be more mature and responsible from here on.

It is important to me to uphold the values of my particular group. I realise that other groups are less vigilant, less disciplined, but then they are not led by my father, they are different: the human notion that all gorilla groups are somehow exactly the same, that one is indistinct from another, is false. Culture is not unique to humans, even though they use this notion to mark themselves out as superior to us, their ape cousins.

Culture is the stamp of humanity, they proclaim, animals do not possess it – they have the unfortunate habit of forgetting that they too are animals – and there is no tribe or nation state that does not claim to have one of its own. And yet it seems to me that humans have used culture, rather erroneously, to distance themselves from their biological roots, origins which are undeniable, despite the powers of delusion they possess, not least because there is evidence of distinct cultures within primate communities: chimpanzees in the Gombe use different tools to fish termites from those used by their contemporaries in other parts of the Congo; and then there are the Bili apes of the magic forest, chimpanzees with a taste for big cat flesh rather than mere termites. Though these cultural differences are slight compared with advanced human cultures, they represent differences nevertheless.

Our father does not interfere with our dispute – for he knows, on this occasion, that it is Kibu alone who is in the wrong. He remains seated in his nest on the forest floor, and just watches while I coax my half brother back up the slope to his sentry position. Kibu walks slowly: he might have given in to the requirements of the group, but this does not mean that he is in a hurry to fulfil them. He will always be a stubborn character, to the very end. It is funny, but humans are sure that, unlike gorillas, they are not biologically and genetically predisposed to behave in the same mindless way day after day – even though my current actions are mindful rather than mindless – and yet it would seem that this is precisely how they do behave most of the time. I am sure that many humans judge gorillas' lives to be exceedingly dull. I mean, what do we do all day other than munch on bland vegetation, meticulously groom one another, snooze in the warm equatorial sun, and mosey slowly, and perhaps rather aimlessly, from one patch of forest to another. Yet could this not be seen as an apt metaphor for their life – the life of a modern human. Humans have far less control, far less independence of thought than they think they do. Life leads them, even though they do their damnedest to lead it.

I stand over Kibu as he takes up his post again at the top of the slope, which looks down over the town below, and only return to my position on the other side when I am sure that he is settled, that he will not give in to his innate rebelliousness once more and abandon his duty. It is true that humans have shown throughout their existence that they can overcome their genes: they can commit to celibacy, which is contrary to their biological drive to reproduce; they can commit suicide at the request of religion, or fight in a war on behalf of their country, contrary to their powerful instinct for survival; and they possess high culture, something which we gorillas do not – literature and art are unique to humans, though this is, of course, only because they possess language. And yet gorillas are also capable of great self-sacrifice: a silverback will give his own life in defence of his family, just as Kibu and I will in defence of ours, as we sit here and keep watch.

But it is humans' powerful need to rise above their ancestors – they possess an almost desperate competitiveness – which gives them a generic chauvinism and arrogance that is hardly appealing. This thought makes me feel threatened, and at this moment I retract my lips and expose my teeth and gums.

I am being negative again, I realise – and I am sorry for this – yet is there not some truth in what I state here? What my father would dismiss as cynicism I would defend as realism. Though Homo sapiens and Gorilla beringei share the same biological and psychological processes – both species are inventive and intelligent, both crave bonding and intimacy, the differences between the two are in degree, not kind – it is the former that constantly needs to assert itself on the world and other species.

I turn my head now, and listen intently to the chirrup of a cricket, this noise captivating me. It sounds almost plaintive. Perhaps it mourns what I do, the persistent human need to dominate.

17

But I am not allowed to go straight home. Instead I am taken somewhere else, I do not know where. Two government soldiers hand me over to an old man with a thick white beard. 'My name is Dilolo,' he says to me, 'and you are going to stay here for a bit so we can help you get better.'

'But I just want to go home to my mother and father.'

'In time, child, in time,' he says quietly, then offers me his hand.

I do not take it, perhaps I cannot trust him, I think, so just follow him.

Dilolo leads me into a big outhouse, which has a metal roof, brick walls and is painted all white. It is very light in here, which makes me feel happy because the bush was always so dark. It is a dormitory, there are maybe twenty beds, and it is clean, so clean it smells of disinfectant, but I like this smell after the dirt of the bush.

'This will be your bed,' he says, pointing to one at the back of the room, and I walk over and stare down at it. It has a pillow, clean white sheets and a blanket. I do not say anything, but just smile. Seeing this makes me very happy. I want to lie down on it right away and sleep forever.

'And these are your clothes,' he goes on, handing me a pair of blue trousers, a white shirt and a pair of underpants.

'Now let me show you where the washrooms are. I want you to take off those filthy old clothes and give yourself a good clean. The nurse will help you,' Dilolo finishes off.

'I do not need her help,' I say quickly.

Looking down at my wounded leg, which is now twice as big as the other one and thick with old, dried blood, he says, 'I think you do.'

The nurse enters and motions me to follow her, which I do. She looks like my old school matron. She is short and plump, with big cheeks and a bottom as large as an elephant's.

The washrooms are brand new, and there are six showers. 'Take off your clothes and sit over there,' she says, handing me a towel.

I take off my clothes, wrap the towel around my waist, and sit down on a small wooden bench.

'I'm going to shave your head, get rid of all the lice. Then I'm going to clean your leg, it might sting a bit, but don't worry,' she continues.

The nurse cuts my hair with scissors, then uses a razor and shaves my scalp until I am completely bald, my head as smooth as an egg.

Next she turns her attention to my leg. She does not use water and blackjack like in the bush, but rather a clear liquid from a bottle that smells really bad and makes me cough. She wets my leg with it, and I watch as she puts some cotton wool to my skin and washes away all the blood until all I can see are a few deep holes.

'You have some shrapnel in your leg that I am going to have to take out, otherwise your leg will become badly infected,' she says.

She uses an instrument with two big pincers like a giant beetle, pulling tiny bits of metal from the holes in my leg. This hurts a lot.

'All done,' she finally says. 'I want you to shower, give yourself a very good clean, and then I will put some dressing on your leg and bandage it up.'

The water is hot, I realise, as I put my hand underneath the showerhead. I have only bathed with water like this a few times, and I worry that it might burn my skin, but it feels nice on it. I stand under the shower and let the water pour onto my head, over my shoulders, down my chest and back, until it forms trails like narrow streams running down my legs. Next I take the soap – it is a new bar and it is bright pink, which I must unwrap first – and rub it all over my body until it forms a thick white foam, my whole body like a small cloud. I scrub my skin with a brush, doing it hard, all the dirt slowly falling away until my skin feels clean and smooth. And finally, I lift my head up, open my eyes and let the water pour onto my face and down my body. I watch as all the soap is washed away.

I turn the shower off, then shake my head and body like a dog that has just been swimming and wants to get dry. I dry myself down with the towel, the nurse comes back and bandages up my leg, then tells me that I must clean my gums and brush my teeth. It has been so long since I have done this. I brush quite hard, and also use a toothpick that I put in between each of my teeth. My gums start to bleed and she tells me that this is normal, that this will happen for some time until my teeth and gums get used to being cleaned again.

'Get dressed now,' the nurse says, 'put on your new clothes.' I put these on and they feel good. It is nice to be so clean after always being dusty and dirty. 'And bring your old clothes with you,' she finishes off.

I walk with her to a small courtyard where lots of other boys and girls are. They are playing different games. I have not played for a long time, have just had to carry things and fight.

A tall, skinny woman approaches me and says, 'Hello Kibwe, my name is Liana.' She has big eyes and high cheekbones.

I do not say anything back to her, just nod.

'Now all of you,' she shouts, 'I want you to welcome Kibwe,' and I look round to see a lot of different faces all staring at me, some smiling and some not.

'All these boys and girls were also abducted by the guerrillas,' she continues. 'Now Kibwe, when a new person joins us at the rehabilitation centre the first thing we ask them to do is to burn their clothes, the clothes they wore in the bush.'

I watch as Dilolo lights a fire and all the children gather round it in a circle. I stand beside Liana with my smelly old clothes in my arms. We watch the fire as it grows, the flames becoming bigger and brighter until it almost seems like they are dancing.

'Now throw them in,' Liana says, 'and let them burn,' and I do as she says. 'And the vessel round your neck. You don't have to be scared any more.' I throw this in the fire as well. 'Watch them, Kibwe, watch them go up in smoke. You will be safe now, here with us.'

I hear the words of a man then, with a deep voice, he is a priest. He says a prayer and asks us to repeat each line after him, next takes my hand and says, 'Accept Jesus Christ as your saviour.'

And I do, I say, 'Jesus Christ is my saviour.'

'Look at the fire, Kibwe,' he goes on. 'It consumes everything, all the badness of your life with the guerrillas. War is without mercy, but Jesus Christ is full of mercy.'

When he has finished I feel very tired, and ask Liana if I can go and sleep. She says yes. I am excited about lying down on the bed. I have not slept on a mattress for a long time.

It is not yet dark, and I am the only one in the dormitory. I pull back the sheets, lie down, and let my head sink into the pillow, it is so soft. Next I pull the blanket up to my chin and feel the warmth, my body feeling snug underneath it. I close my eyes and listen to my breathing. I soon fall asleep.

∽

I wake up in the middle of the night to what I think is the sound of gunfire. I sit up in bed, breathing deeply, thinking the guerrillas have come for me, clutching the blanket to my chest.

'It is okay, it is okay,' the boy next to me says, 'it is just the rain,' and with these words I realise that this is all it is, just the heavy patter of rain on the metal roof of the dormitory.

'Thank you,' I whisper to him, then lie back down again and try and get my breath back.

In the morning I follow the rest of the boys in my dormitory to the dining room, where we are given a breakfast of eggs and flatbread. I eat it very slowly because it is wonderful to taste food like this after so much sorghum and nothing else.

'How are we this morning, Kibwe?' Dilolo asks, putting his hand on my shoulder. 'Did you sleep well?'

'Yes, I did. Thank you,' I reply.

'Have you started to get to know some of the other boys in your dormitory?' he goes on, and as he says this the boy who sleeps next to me, the one who told me it was okay when it was just raining, smiles at me from across the table. Dilolo spots this and says, 'Ah, so I see you have met Arron. He is just trouble,' and laughs then, and Arron joins him. 'He has been with us about three months,' Dilolo says. 'When he first came, he was like you, all skin and bone. We had to feed him up. But look at him now, how big and strong he is.'

'Soon I will be bigger than you, uncle,' Arron declares.

'You will never be as big as me,' Dilolo replies, patting his belly, 'at least I hope not,' and this makes me smile. 'Arron was quiet like you when he first arrived here. Now he will not shut up.'

'Thanks uncle,' Arron quips.

'Listen Kibwe, if you want or need anything, let me know.'

'I will,' I answer, and realise how strange this place seems to me. The people here are so kind, so caring. They are nothing like the guerrillas.

∞

I begin to like life in the centre. They tell me that my parents know I am safe, and that I will be home with them soon. We do not study here, it is not a school. They want us to have fun, they say, to be children again after being made to be like adults. I start to have happy moments again, I laugh, something which I have not done for a long time. Also I begin to play lots of football with the other boys, and Arron is very good. I think he could play for a big team in Europe.

There is a joke here, that once you are fat enough they let you go home. Some of the food they give us I have not tasted before. It comes out of a tin can, and is usually either corned beef or tuna. We also eat lots of vegetables like sweet potato and plantain. These two are my favourites because they are both sweet. And instead of posho or sorghum they give us macaroni, which I had not tasted before I came here but like a lot. They also allow us to have one bottle of soda a week, and I always choose Coca Cola. I bring it straight to my mouth, yank off the top with my teeth, guzzle it all down in one go, then do a loud burp straight after.

I find myself getting angrier as the weeks go on, so angry that my face often goes red, my chest feels tight, my head starts humming and spinning with lots of thoughts, and I just want to hurt someone. But I never act on these thoughts, thank God. Some of the boys do fight each other, but they are immediately made to stop and told they must not use violence any more, now they are no longer guerrillas. They must find other ways to solve arguments, to make things better.

One older boy tells me how, when he gets angry, a thing just seems 'to go click' in his head and he wants to hit or stab the person who has made him feel this way. This is what he used to do when he was a guerrilla, just hit out whenever he felt bad. But now he must 'try very hard to be calm and reasonable,' he says, 'to understand different people and situations'.

Every week I see a woman called Helene for one hour, and I am meant to talk to her and tell her how I am feeling. It is strange to talk a lot after so much silence in the bush, and it makes my mouth ache a bit. When I first start talking the words that come out of my mouth do not seem to be mine – they seem alien to me even though they are mine. In the beginning I do not want to tell her the angry thoughts I am having because I am ashamed of them and she might think badly of me. The thoughts make me feel like a bad person, and they scare me because they are often so strong. Why should I want to hurt people? And why should I be having these harmful thoughts now, now that I am free from the guerrillas? I ask myself these questions, and many others. I should be feeling happy and peaceful.

But one week when I am with Helene I suddenly get mad at her and I imagine myself reaching over, grabbing her by the throat and trying to strangle her, kill her. She sees my face going red and says, 'You are angry, Kibwe, I can see.'

'No I am not!' I shout, and because I react like this she knows that I am.

'Is there something you want to tell me?' she asks.

'Yes,' I reply sadly, and then tell her about some of the horrible thoughts I am having. She looks at me very closely when I say this stuff, like she is studying me, and I worry she will not want to talk to me again once I am finished and will just have me locked up and never let out.

'Kibwe, it is okay,' she finally says, 'you are very angry at the moment. You could not be angry when you were with the guerrillas, you were not allowed to feel. Your feelings are coming out again, that is all, and this is a big shock to you because a lot of them are very powerful and frightening. They are like this because of what you have been through, what they made you do. And so now you are angry with everyone and want to hit out, get your own back. I would be feeling the same way as you, having the same thoughts, if I were you.'

I go on to tell her more things, about how I killed one man and shot another, about the cruelty of Kola, about the bad things that Captain Djeke did, and about all the terrible things that I saw Commander Kalango do.

When I have finished speaking she just takes me in her arms and holds me, holds me tight, I feel her chin on my shoulder, and it is lovely to be held by her. This makes me think of my mother, how she used to hold me.

∞

They have a parliament here, which meets on Tuesdays and Fridays, and lasts three hours, from ten in the morning until one o'clock in the afternoon. If you have any problems you raise these in the parliament. They want you to talk about things instead of fighting over them. Liana says there is too much fighting in the world, especially in Africa, and she wants us to learn to fight with words and feelings instead of with machetes and guns.

I carry on seeing Helene every week, and she helps me better understand how the guerrillas stole my childhood from me, made me do things that children are not supposed to do. I like it that she listens to me, and also reassures me. She says, 'It is not your right to kill someone, but you must understand, Kibwe, that you were made to kill, you were given no choice.'

But today I am feeling low, bad about myself, and so do not want to hear what she is saying. 'I could have refused to kill!' I shout.

'But then they would have killed you,' she says, and even though I know she is right I find it hard to accept. 'They made you a man-child, Kibwe, a victim who became a victimiser, who made more victims.'

'I am worried what will happen if they take me again. General Mushamuka can probably see me now. You see, they put the medicine on me.'

'Forget the medicine! Mushamuka does not have special powers to see you, he is not the Devil, just a very bad man,' Helene insists.

I am just silent.

As the weeks continue to go by and become months, I find that the more I talk to her the more I dream. They are bad at first, just nightmares – me forcing myself on the girl, me beating Kisunga, me grabbing the old woman by the neck, me shooting the government soldier and his blood going everywhere as he chokes and dies. These images flash through my mind, go round and round, sometimes seem to be in my head all night, and I cannot get rid of them. And it is like the more I want them to go away the more they stay and keep on tormenting me. But Helene helps me to cry, I trust her now, and though sometimes I feel like I am going mad, the more I tell her about the nightmares, the images in my head, the better I feel. I also start to say prayers with her for the man I killed and the other I shot. I say sorry to them and ask for their forgiveness, even though I am not with them, even though they are not here any more.

I make friends with one girl, Lulu. She is younger than me, just ten. The guerrillas did very bad things to her. They raped her and shoved things inside her, bits of iron and nails. She does not look at me when she tells me this, holds her head tilted to one side, and speaks in a very soft and quiet voice, almost like a whisper.

But the more we talk, the more she is able to look at me, and the louder her voice becomes, until she finally smiles, I see her cheeks crease, her lips spread, her mouth open, her white teeth glint at me. The smile does not

NICK TAUSSIG

last long, but she is happy, yes, if only for a split second.
She will get better, she will be okay, I think.

And yet there are others here who are never going to be okay, never going to be able to go back to a normal life. Most of these are the older ones, the ones who spent far longer than me in the bush – five, six, seven years. These boys and girls are sixteen, seventeen and eighteen, and there is a deep pain and sadness in them that is too big to ever go away.

I realise that the best thing about this place is that I am no longer treated like an animal. No, I am cared for like a living person – I get love. I lost hope in the bush, but now I have it back.

18

The air is soporific; I lounge in a tree, on my own, some way off from the rest of the group. I hear a melancholic whine, and turn to see a young bushbuck flailing on the ground. I hear the screams of monkeys. Like apes and other animals they possess empathy. Poachers must be near, I realise. I hurry over.

It is a female, and she is caught in a neck-rope noose: she must have been browsing for blackberries. This trap, designed to catch antelope, is triggered by the head of the browsing animal, and once the noose is round the head the antelope is slowly strangled to death.

I reach for her head, wedge it underneath my arm, then pull at the wire noose with my canines until it is loose enough for me to get my fingers underneath, then pull it over her neck with my hands: my father taught me this – he has rescued many antelope – and I remember now how he finally freed my mother.

Her heart beats against the side of my chest: it beats frantically, I feel the ebb and flow of blood coursing through her. As soon as I let go of her head she jumps forward, out of my grasp. It is okay, I signal to her, trying to calm and reassure her.

She looks at me at this moment, her brown eyes so soft, the colour of her fur, then nods her head in gratitude, which prompts me to admire her neck, so willowy. I smile at her, and she stands still, her eyes resting on me. And then she is gone, darting off into the forest once more.

Dogs barking…the poachers must be close now… they must have heard the antelope's whine, as I did. Three rush towards me, snarling, baring their teeth. I rise up and stand on my legs, this gesture, I hope, making it clear to them that I am not afraid, that I will not tolerate their threats.

They are silent almost immediately, glance at one another, then scamper off, back into virgin forest.

The rest of the group must know about the trap I just discovered, that poachers and their dogs are nearby. I hurry off to inform them.

It saddens me, why humans have such an insatiable appetite for hunting. I know why, of course I do – they are highly predatory, the dominant species. And yet the brutality with which they kill almost belies their intelligence. A human has a large neocortex like a gorilla does, and an even larger frontal lobe. In fact, the human brain is double the size of a gorilla's of equivalent body size. And so they judge us to be unintelligent: we might be capable of some rational thought, but this ability is very limited when compared to theirs, they conclude. Humans have a standard of intelligence, and seek to apply this cross-species, even though such a means of assessment is likely to produce a false conclusion. And yet this does not matter. For as long as the measurement proves them to be dominant, then they are content.

But sadly, despite their great intelligence, humans are also very destructive and will stop at nothing to protect and fulfil themselves, albeit at the expense of other animals, many of whom, including my species, are now threatened with extinction. If only their virtue were proportionate to their intelligence: their higher level of intentionality, their greater imagination, does not make them nobler, more compassionate.

Heading down one of the main trails, past thickets of brambles, I am not far from the group now. I can see Lisala swinging from a liana. It looks like she is trying to build up enough momentum to reach a high branch on an adjacent tree, what looks like a Faurea saligna. She must have spotted some food there. Like her father and elder brother, she is willing to go to great lengths in order to satisfy her appetite. Humans have performed an infinite number of theory-of-mind tests on gorillas, but do not suppose that we score low on many of them – we demonstrate no more than second- or third-order intentionality – only because we cannot quite see the point of such tests. Unlike them, we are not obsessed with intelligence. We realise it does not bring happiness, and that there are other attributes which are just as, if not more, important. It is also worth noting that we live in a markedly different environment to humans, where physical, rather than mental, prowess is far more important: we are better equipped to survive in the depths of the forest than they are.

The popular belief among humans is that chimpanzees are more intelligent than gorillas, possess greater cognitive machinery: they use many tools; their groups are larger than ours. However, we have less need for tools than they do, principally because we are vegetarian and do not have a penchant for termites. And the size of our groups, well, because we are a sexually dimorphic species – the male twice the size of the female – and are wary of politics, we live in far smaller groups than our ape cousins. Chimpanzees are like humans – competitive and aggressive, ambitious and political beings obsessed with power – and male power politics continues to dominate their societies, rich in machination and provocation, power maintained by the forceful assertion of dominance, violence always implicit, if not explicit, in this assertion. Compared to chimpanzees we gorillas are almost apolitical. But this might explain why humans rate them more intelligent than us: they see themselves so clearly in them. It is as if they are looking in a mirror. We, on the other hand, are rather more transparent and straightforward; our relationships with one another are less complex, and there is perhaps an honesty and purity to them which human and chimpanzee relationships lack.

I am directly beneath Lisala now, and can at last see what she was after – bracket fungus. She sits on the branch of the adjacent tree and savours her discovery, pouting her lips, opening her mouth and chewing excitedly, seeming to smack her stomach in anticipation of it being filled. And then she swallows, the fungus sliding down her throat and entering her stomach, and I hear her sigh, this sound expressing deep contentment. I do not think she has seen me.

Human lineage is deeply embedded within the great ape family, specifically the African great ape family. The comparisons between Homo sapiens and Pan troglodytes are, indeed, striking. The former shares ninety-nine percent of the latter's active genetic material – humans are more closely related to chimpanzees than gorillas – and both species are full of anger, always struggling to control this emotion. Both are also strongly territorial and prone to xenophobia, valuing the lives of those within their group more than the lives of those outside it. And both are predisposed to respond favourably to mass indoctrination and harsh authority, though a human's proclivity to be brainwashed and governed is far greater than a chimp's. In truth, humans thrive under authoritarian rule and can descend, quite easily, into mass psychopathology, willing to participate in genocide for the benefit of one particular group versus another. This is rather ironic, not least in the context of modern human culture, which celebrates independence of thought. Humans and chimpanzees, it seems, would be wise to look to their bonobo cousin, Pan paniscus, for inspiration, a more egalitarian, free-spirited and peace-loving species, though let me stress not quite as virtuous as humans first thought.

Lisala takes her last mouthful of fungus, then gently lies back on the branch she sits on, putting her hands behind her head and seeming to revel, and lose herself, in the satisfaction she now feels as her legs dangle lazily either side of her, like they are floating on air. She will savour this feeling, it is clear. We gorillas are free of illusion, and treat the world as we experience it: in the latter respect we are like children, and in the former like wise old men. If only all humans – not just their children and their old – would follow our example rather than blunder blindly on.

Perhaps this is the species' undoing, its relentless striving. I run my hand over my brow, open and close my eyes. I am tired, my head hurts. Why cannot humans just see, observe and experience things as they are? It seems they are unable to live wholly in the here and now. We gorillas are better at experiencing the world as it is. To this extent, we are maybe more in touch with reality. Only a handful of humans can live as we do, in the present moment, and they are referred to as 'enlightened beings'. If only gorillas were referred to with such reverence.

Continuing to look up at Lisala and admire her, my beautiful little sister, I finally question bark, notifying her of my presence. She is not startled. Perhaps she has known all this time that I have been standing beneath her, watching her. She simply lifts her head and smiles at me, her face illuminated by the sun that now hangs huge and red in the sky.

19

It is a weird feeling when the airplane lifts off the ground. I stare out of the window, down at the grass and trees below, everything becoming smaller. Though I am strapped into my seat I want to stand up, lift my arms up either side of my body and pretend I am a bird, that I am flying. This is my first time in an airplane, and it is very exciting.

The plane suddenly dips, my stomach goes up and down like it does when I am about to be sick, and we shake from side to side. I grab hold of the seat in front quite hard, but the man sitting next to me says, 'You do not need to do that, you know, you are quite safe. This is only a bit of turbulence.'

'Really?' I ask him, holding my tummy and waiting for the sick feeling to pass.

'Yes, the pilot knows what he is doing, I have flown with him before. In fact, he often flies much bigger planes than this.'

'There are bigger ones?'

'Yes, far bigger. The plane we are in today is a very small one.'

We do not fly for long, no more than about an hour, and land in a field. Looking out of the window, I see that it is the field next to my school. I am finally home.

When I step out of the plane and into the bright of the midday sun I see my father. He runs over, grabs me, and holding me tight pushes my head against his chest and holds it there, clinging to me, breathing deeply, and saying my name over and over, 'Kibwe…Kibwe… Kibwe…Kibwe.'

I hear his voice wobble and croak a bit – I have never seen my father cry, and if he is crying at this moment, he will not let me see.

'Our village is still not safe,' he says after a bit, his voice sounding more like it normally does, strong and deep. 'We remain in the camp. Let me take you to your mother,' and he pulls away from me, puts his hand on my shoulder and says, 'Let's go.'

We walk home, and I cannot wait to see her.

My father calls to my mother inside the banda, saying, 'Look who is here. Look who is here.'

When I first see her face as she hurries from the dark of the hut into the light of day I am struck by how much older she looks. It has been less than two years, and yet for my mother it is more like a decade. She smiles, the lines around her eyes deep-set and thick, her hair now shot through with streaks of grey. She puts her hands to my face and stares hard into my eyes, as if she is searching for something, desperate to make sure that it is really me, her son. 'I was praying so hard that you would come back. And you have, here you are, my precious Kibwe,' and she holds me then, and I let myself sink into her arms, and we both slide to the ground on our knees and stay like this for a long time, holding one another.

It is hard to see her again. I had told myself not to think about her when I was in the bush because it made me so sad. And yet here I now am, with her again, in her arms. 'Will you stop crying, please?' I finally say to her. 'I am alive, not dead. You do not need to cry. I do not want you to suffer any more.'

'I'm sorry, I'm sorry,' she says. 'It is just that during those darker days I was sure you were dead, that my prayers were falling on deaf ears. But you are alive, yes, and I will stop now...I will stop crying.'

'Have you kept my school uniform?' I ask her.

'Yes, of course I have.'

'So I can go to school in the morning, then come back in the afternoon and help you? I can dig sweet potato, bring cassava.'

'Yes, you can,' she replies, wiping her eyes with the tips of her fingers. 'Your father and I planted a small crop not too long ago after the guerrillas had raided it and taken everything.'

My father continues to work the small piece of land at the back of the camp. He goes every morning at sunrise and works through to midday, and then he returns late in the afternoon and works until sunset. He does this to keep his dignity, he says. Back in the village, he had his own cattle, his own crops, he could feed himself and his family. But now he, like every other man in the camp, depends on the World Food Programme to feed his family, and himself.

As the sun sets, members of my clan gather round my banda. There are about thirty of them. Oleé is among them, I am happy to see him. His mother is dead, I learn. The disease killed her. They carry food and water, which means they have forgiven me, do not blame me for being a guerrilla. I am no longer their enemy. There is posho, groundnut sauce, simsim paste, sweet potato. Before we eat, my father speaks, addressing everyone.

'Life here in the camps is difficult. We have spent too long away from our village, our homes, too long relying on the World Food Programme, too long living in fear of the guerrillas, too long unable to cultivate our own food and produce food for others.

'And our children have suffered greatly. The boys have been abducted, the girls have been raped. They are despondent, many of them unable to attend school because we cannot afford to send them. And so many resort to alcohol and prostitution.

'Yet we must never stop trying to overcome these problems. We must not become despondent, we must continue to strive to be productive, we must have hope.

'Kibwe, you have returned from the bush, and we thank God for this, that He delivered you safely back to us. For death can come at any time. You have given us hope!'

My father then says grace and asks everyone to eat. When I stop he tells me to eat more, but I cannot, my stomach is not used to so much food.

I must use the toilet. It is towards the back of the camp, is shared by hundreds of us, this stinking hole in the ground, and makes me want to retch. I piss as quickly as I can, as flies buzz around me, then leave.

As I hurry out I am confronted by a man I knew from before. His name is Nkan and he does not like me. He is from another clan. He holds a bottle of beer in his hand, he stumbles a bit, he is drunk. 'You, boy, you do not deserve all this attention. You should be punished, not forgiven. The moment they took you, you became one of them, a guerrilla. You are bad now!'

And he scowls at me, his eyes like glass, spits down at my feet, next pushes me in the chest, and I feel myself getting angry, like I did in the centre, my chest tightening, but I do not want him to see this.

'I must stay cool…I must stay cool,' I mutter to myself.

Boys gather round Nkan, boys from his clan, some older than me and some younger. He carries on, pointing at me, 'This one, he is a guerrilla. He stole from us, he hurt us, he killed us. He cannot be trusted, he cannot be forgiven. He must be punished!'

The boys start shouting at me, calling me terrible names like 'thief', 'guerrilla', 'murderer' and 'devil', and my bad thoughts suddenly return and I imagine shooting them all with my Aka, even though I do not have it any more. They punch and kick me until I fall to the ground, and then just keep on punching and kicking. It is as if there are hundreds of them, and there is nothing I can do other than roll up in a ball and try and protect my head.

'Stop it! Stop it!' I hear my father's cries as he pulls boys off me. 'Nkan, we might be from rival clans, but here, in this Godforsaken place, we are all one. We are just trying to survive until the war ends, until the guerrillas stop fighting.'

'Leave him!' Nkan blurts out, and the boys suddenly stop.

'Kibwe, are you okay?' my father asks urgently, kneeling down by my side.

'I got used to beatings like this in the bush,' I say quietly, and he helps me to my feet.

I walk slowly with my father back to our banda. I am not badly hurt. He makes sure I am okay, then goes off to see his sister, my auntie, while I sit inside with my mother. We sit in the dark and I listen to her breath.

'What did they make you do?' she asks, stroking my feet, the skin so rough now, hardened by the bush. Maybe Helene has told her everything. Maybe my mother thinks my heart has become worn like my feet.

At first, I want to tell her that I did nothing bad, that I did not kill anyone, but then I realise this is not the right thing to do, that I should tell her, that like Helene she will hopefully be able to understand why I did what I did. And so I tell my mother, just like I told Helene.

'Look at me,' I say to her when I have finished talking. She holds her head in her hands.

'Give me a moment, Kibwe,' she mumbles.

'I am still your son,' I insist.

'I know,' she says, and then lifts her head from her hands. She looks at me differently now, but not in the way that Nkan did, rather with sadness in her eyes, that her son has been forced to do such things at such a young age. She looks at me as if I am no longer a child but a grown-up.

'But now I am not a guerrilla any more, now I am free, I am going to be a good son to you and I am going to study hard, and if I pass into senior school then I will work, I will dig cassava, make bricks, do all the things I need to do in order to pay the fees. I would like to be a teacher one day.'

'And you will be, Kibwe, you will be,' and she smiles at me.

I wait for her to close her eyes, then make my bed underneath the stars. I feel safe. The government soldiers are watching over us and my father is close by. It is warm and the stars are glowing.

20

My father urges me to head west: he knows this area of the forest well. There I might find a little more sympathy in my heart for humans: he worries that my growing anger and bitterness with them is consuming me. I must draw on my 'inherited wisdom', he stresses yet again, this notion which my father has so much conviction in – his faith perhaps. I am reluctant to go, but he insists, and I cannot refuse him.

It is a cold morning; clouds loom large and heavy in the sky. I walk for a long time, and wonder whether my father is simply punishing me for my pessimism.

But then I see it, beyond the forest, beyond the grassland and wildflowers, a camp full of humans living in terrible squalor: he has told me of the destitution that some humans live in, but to actually see this with my own eyes is shocking. We gorillas are sometimes judged harshly for how we treat one another: silverbacks are prone to occasional displays of violence, crashing through undergrowth and deliberately running down innocent groups of females and young; however, peace is always quickly restored as soon as male honour is satisfied. But we would never display the level of intraspecies disregard and contempt I see before me now. How poorly this species sometimes cares for its own: it is almost beyond comprehension.

This is one of the internal displacement camps – my father has witnessed many of them – and the situation here is dire. When the villagers were driven out of their homes by the guerrillas, they lost their livelihood and, even more significantly, their very way of life. There are some four thousand people here, according to my father, and across the country some two million languishing in camps such as this, reliant on the World Food Programme and forced to do little more than live from one day to the next, quietly hoping that the war will end so they can return to their homesteads, their villages. The battle to preserve one's dignity under such harsh circumstances is great, and yet the battle for survival is greater still.

I decide to move closer, to the very perimeter of the forest, and stand behind a palm tree, one of its giant fronds covering my head, shoulders and saddle. As I look down into the camp it is as if everyone needs help: it is like a ghost town, a place that has had its heart ripped out. All the aid organisations are here: USAID, UNICEF, UNHCR, CPAR, Save the Children, Médecins Sans

Frontières, International Red Cross, World Vision, Caritas and many more. The names and logos of these organisations are omnipresent, even displayed on T-shirts worn by the residents, their attire a strange mix of Western hand-me-downs and traditional African dress. Government soldiers pass by in pickups, and many of them look bored and disaffected: the government pays them little and does not treat them well, but in a country which suffers from chronic unemployment the majority of them are not in a position to look for other work.

When the camps were first constructed – my father remembers when there were none – bandas were thrown up quickly, packed closely together, families forced to live on top of one another. At first they were optional, but then they became compulsory, the government forcing all villagers to leave their homes. These dense populations in confined areas were meant to provide security – the rationale of the government was safety in numbers – and yet they have failed to offer this. Rather, they have offered something close to the opposite: the camps' inhabitants, when confronted by guerrillas with guns, have been able to do little more than beg for mercy, and for their lives. The President will not permit the people to arm themselves, as he might then suffer the same fate that he inflicted on his predecessor: national resistance and revolution. He remains woefully consistent with the majority of African leaders: he is unable to relinquish power.

And thus it is now as if the camps simply afford the guerrillas bigger stages on which to commit their atrocities: they have become grotesque amphitheatres of murder and mayhem. And when the inhabitants are not terrorised by guerrillas they are terrorised by disease – malaria and cholera are rife – and hunger. The bellies of most of the children protrude, the eyes red and sunken, and thick with mucus, the heads swollen, all symptoms of malnutrition, flies cramming into their eyes and around their mouths as if in preparation for their deaths. A human body dying from starvation cannibalises itself, quite literally.

Clouds swirl above me at this moment, the wind carrying them towards the camp – they are low and opaque, and the light that filters through them sallow and critical – and when they reach it, their end destination it seems, they paint the whole place grey, desperate and despondent. I want to leave this place, for I am feeling gloomy, but then how can I not feel this way when there is evidence of so much suffering. Some of the camp's inhabitants ask for whatever help can be given, while others, it appears, have simply given up asking. Western charities make occasional visits: some come with footballs for the children, others with incidentals such as soap, toothbrushes and toothpaste. And yet the former end up being sold for booze – many of the camp elders can do little more than drown their sorrows – while the latter are often traded for food, which takes priority over hygiene and dental health.

I need to defecate, and leave the shelter of the palm tree, temporarily. Sex might be the great opiate of the Western world, and yet those in the camp cannot even find pleasure and distraction here: AIDS is rife, and in a country which still clings to Christianity as its route to salvation and, it seems, civilisation – tribal society continues to be judged as something primitive, even bestial – abstinence is promoted rather than safe sex. It could be argued that this kind of atavism, more than war, is the greatest killer of all in Africa, and much of the promotion of abstinence is done not by the government but rather by foreign NGOs: Africa remains a missionary heartland, its people very responsive to the word of Jesus Christ. When will Christianity be able to accept, once and for all, that man is a highly sexual animal and that the suppression of this powerful, intrinsic drive is fruitless: the man cannot be taken out of man! He likes to fuck. I would never think that I could change human's sexual behaviour, just as I could never hope to change bonobo's. Like Homo sapiens, this other primate species is also obsessed with sex.

But then, resuming my observation, under the cover of the same palm, I see the children – a large group of them have assembled on a patch of grassland not far from the camp, under the watchful eye of a few government soldiers – and they start to skip, jump and chase one another, their boundless energy reminding me of my two juvenile half brothers, who likewise seem to be able to engage in never-ending play. And at this moment the clouds above them start spitting rain, light at first, then heavy. The massive frond above my head provides me with shelter, though I do not need it: it rains over the camp only. I watch the children as they start to head for the muddy ground to the right of the camp, where puddles form quickly and ditches fill with water. They accumulate more mud on their bare bodies the nearer they get, and when they reach their intended destination they hurl themselves in the ditches, splashing water over themselves and others. Like elephants bathing in a water hole, they revel in the mud and the wet, overcome by an urgent sense of play. The adults behind them merely look on impassively, but my despair lifts as I continue to watch them. For they possess such hope and resilience that I feel if anything is to defeat Mushamuka and his guerrillas, it is the spirit of these children.

My father will now be worrying about me: I have been here some time, and should start making my way back. And so, with this in mind, I lift the frond from the top of my head, my palm disguise, and it trails down my saddle as I walk away from the camp into the dense forest again.

21

I am woken early by the cockerel, singing the morning as loud as he can. I used to be able to sleep through all his singing, but not any more. He is joined by the gentle bleating of a small goat.

I get up and decide to go for a walk through the camp, and it is as quiet as the bush at this time of day.

The sun rises slowly, like it is not sure it wants to start the day, its rays a pale yellow.

Things are still the same, little has changed since I have been away.

I look down at my bare feet as they move one in front of the other, my toes getting redder from the devils of dust on the hard beaten ground. There is no grass – nothing grows here. They make everything red, my clothes and skin, and I remember how me and Oleé, when we used to play by the roadside, would close our eyes when a car went by. If we did not do this, then dust would get inside, making them blink and itch. We closed our mouths as well, otherwise we would cough and splutter. And when we finally opened our eyes again, all we could ever see was a thick haze of dust in the air like a swarm of red locusts, the car no longer visible beyond it.

Ahead of me now I see sorghum, ochra and groundnuts spread out on mats in the early morning sun. Beans soak in plastic bowls outside bandas. I see a woman standing over a big stove of boiling water. She will sell this water. Here, clean water has a price. This is what Mr Bayona says.

The food that the World Food Programme provides is not enough to sustain us, just sorghum, and occasionally beans. I think about the food they gave us in the centre, the corned beef and tuna, the sweet potato and plantain. There will be none of these here. Meat is a luxury. The few goats provide milk, they are not to be eaten. We can get dried fish, which is sold in a small market at the front of the camp. It does not taste as good as goat or chicken. I ate lots of it before I was abducted. I have always hated its smell.

I am near the other side of the camp. I see an elderly man sitting outside his banda watching the sunrise. He is drunk. I watch him hit his dog. The animal yelps, then runs away. There must still be a lot of drinking here, I think. My mother used to tell me 'it is because the people are bored'. They have had their lives taken away from them. 'It is very difficult to keep your pride living in a place like this,' she would say, just like my father. 'Some men become so frustrated that they end up just fighting each other, then go home and hit their wives and children.'

I make my way back to my banda. My mother is awake. She asks me if I can go into town and pick up another jerrycan. One of hers has a hole in it.

Standing at the roadside, I look out for a boda-boda. Whenever I went into town before I would normally hitch a ride. I enjoyed this, it was always fun and bumpy, and I loved the feel of the wind against my cheeks as we sped down the long, dusty road. But I cannot see one now, and so decide to walk.

When I finally arrive, a big ceremony is getting under way. It is a fertility one. There are lots of very pretty girls dancing, gyrating to the beats of tom-toms. I stand and watch them, their beautiful backs and shoulders shining in the midday sun, and I start to lose my mind to the beat, boom-boom … boom-boom … boom-boom … boom-boom, and close my eyes, rock my head and shake my body. I think maybe I can stay here forever with this music because I like it so much. I dance until I am tired, until my legs ache and feel floppy, until the drumbeats stop.

I get the jerrycan, then make the long walk back. I join my mother and father at the small piece of land at the back of the camp. We dig another patch and plant cassava. I remember how much land we had before in our village. One year the locusts came and destroyed some of our crop, reducing a whole field of millet to short stumps within minutes. And yet still we had enough food. We could not survive such a fate now, we have such a small area to farm on.

∞

The next morning I go back to school. I walk with all the other children from the camp. We are escorted by government soldiers. They are here to protect us, to make sure we are safe from the guerrillas. I am so happy to be here, with my friends once more.

I have to go in a class with children younger than me in order to catch up on all that I have missed, but I do not mind doing this, especially since it means that Mr Bayona will still be my teacher.

I really enjoy my first day back, and Mr Bayona is very kind to me and makes me laugh a lot.

When school finishes the government soldiers are there to escort us back to the camp. And it is as we walk back that we see the fires, then hear the screams and the cries…the guerrillas have returned.

I immediately sense that my mother and father are in danger, and so I start to run. One of the soldiers with us calls me back, but I do not listen to him, I just keep going, run as fast as I can.

I am in the camp now and heading for my banda. Guerrillas are everywhere, there are at least one hundred of them. I try and see if I can recognise any of them. I see one from a distance and think it is Kola, he is right by my banda, but when I get closer I realise it is not him. My mother and father are not there. Perhaps they are working the land, I think, and turn suddenly, my feet skidding on the sandy ground, and run towards the back of the camp.

Someone is chasing me, I can feel him behind me. I turn and spot a Senior on my tail. He carries an Aka.

When I look ahead again it is my father I see first. He kneels on the ground, in the patch of land where we have just planted cassava. A Senior stands over him, holding a gun to his head. I see a woman lying on the ground a few feet away from him, her dress hoisted up, her knickers pulled down around her ankles, her blouse ripped, her breasts bloody. Her head flops to one side as a Senior lifts himself off her, pulls up his trousers and asks, 'Anyone else want a go?' It is my mother. She is silent.

'No!' I scream, and at that moment the Senior with the gun to my father's head turns, looks at me blankly, then fires. I watch my father fall forward, face down on the ground.

'Is this woman your mother?' he demands.

'Yes, please do not hurt her any more.'

'Hurt her? We have not hurt her. We have just fucked her... all of us!' he says, and smiles at me while chewing on a stick of sugar cane, one of his gold front teeth flashing in the late afternoon sun.

I want to charge at him like a buffalo and kill him. I wish I was a big silverback gorilla, I would rip his head off. The Senior who was tailing me thrusts his Aka between my feet, I stumble and fall to the ground, but not before I have managed to hook the gun's shoulder strap round my ankle and pull it away from him and into my own hands. I turn the gun on him, shouting, 'Let my mother go!'

But then there is a thud and I cannot see well, everything becomes blurred and I...

'I should make you kill her,' are the first words I hear as I open my eyes and stare at the gold-toothed Senior, who stands over me, his Aka resting on my forehead. My mother is no longer silent, I can hear her quietly moaning.

Then the other Senior, the one who was chasing me and whose gun I took, says, 'You were a guerrilla, I can see,' and he prods me in the ribs with his Aka. 'Well, you will be one again. We will take you with us.'

'Say goodbye to your mother,' the gold-toothed one says, walks over to her and shoots her three times in the chest.

No sound comes from my mother. I feel a great pain in my own chest, as if I have been shot there as well, then I feel my arms being tugged, my hands pulled behind my back and tied together. I am dragged to my feet and told to move. The two guerrillas lead me off into the bush once more.

Why has God let this happen? *How* can God let this happen?

Again, when I need Him most, He is silent, does not answer me.

22

Grey and black clouds swirl and mass in the sky, the wind whips through the trees – a storm is coming. There is a bad feeling amongst us today. Again, I have clashed with Kibu. Again, my father has reprimanded us both. My mother is tetchy, Lisala unhappy. The whole group is solemn and watchful as we sit on the forest floor, daynesting, huddled around my father. The pressure of what is happening, just beyond the forest, continues to bear down on us evermore.

Until humans began to threaten us with extinction our families were reasonably solid and secure. Yes, they were affected by birth and death and occasional migration, but other than these fundamental traits of gorilla existence families remained together, they prevailed. However, now families are driven apart, as we are being, by poachers in search of bushmeat and trophies; guerrillas in search of their next kill; hungry villagers in search of something to eat; and loggers in search of yet more wood.

Before Homo sapiens came we thrived: millions of us inhabited this great frontier forest we live in, that once extended across the whole continent. But the march of loggers from Europe, and now Asia, is relentless, and though local independent loggers are willing to stop, the big international logging companies are not. At the rate they are going we will not have a home soon.

Getting to my feet, I stand beside my father and belch-grunt, urging him to move the group once more – we must, for our own safety, go deeper into the forest, further away from the humans – and yet he remains adamant that we stay put, that we should not run any more but rather face our fate, and so he stands up on all fours and stares me down, pig-grunting, forcing me into submission as I put my forearms to the ground. I am frightened, not of him though, but of our fate.

Africa remains a continent dominated by one-party states and military dictatorships, ruled by the gun, in post-colonial meltdown, one-fifth of her people living in countries battered by war. In such countries there is little semblance of infrastructure: there are no schools, there is no law and order, the people do not pay taxes. How can they when there are no jobs. State violence and corruption are rife; the public's hatred and distrust grows ever stronger. The cause of democracy and development often seems hopeless in a place so full of passion and rage, in a place so vulnerable to sectarianism and ethnicity, and it is easy for rogue generals and warlords to thrive here, to foment fire and anarchy, to recruit people to loot, rape and kill. Mushamuka is just one of many, a suave but erratic intellectual with a deep love of violence, who claims he is fighting for his people but in reality is fighting for little more than personal wealth and power.

I remain frustrated – I cannot accept my father's decision – and so challenge him again. I walk away from the group, urging Chim and Pumbu to follow me, then look to my two juvenile half brothers, belch-grunting at them as well.

My father immediately looks over at me, his annoyance clear enough, brow furrowed, eyes holding my stare. And yet I do not submit to his will, and get back down on the forest floor, but rather stand my ground, push my chest out and hold my head high.

He moves swiftly, without hesitation, perceiving my defiance as a direct threat to his authority. He pig-grunts, roars, and charges at me, baring his teeth.

I am no match for my father, and find myself, almost instinctively, cowering. I know that he would not bite me, know that he would not hurt me, and he knows that I know this, and this is perhaps why the look that he gives me at this moment is so full of disappointment – that I have driven him to become so angry, forced him to challenge me in this way, in front of the rest of the group. And yet still, even in spite of this, I feel he has not made the right choice, and must be made to think again.

Close to extinction, Mushamuka and the guerrillas know our value. Thus, if the President does not leave them be, afford them sanctuary with us in the forest, then they will kill us, kill us all. We are strategic pawns in their feud, that is all.

And so is it not ironic, in light of this, that humans find it so very difficult to admit that they are driven by power, that power is perhaps their greatest aphrodisiac. Maybe this is because this dominant aspect of their nature conflicts with the principal image they have of themselves as virtuous, benign and egalitarian. If only they would be more honest: for they are also bad, malignant and repressive. And these negative aspects cannot simply be got rid of: for they are as much a part of them as the virtuous ones. Rather, humans would do well to view themselves for what they actually are: highly evolved bipedal apes obsessed with power and sex, and with a dangerous sense of their own importance that ought to be constantly reigned in.

I remain standing. My father looks, first, to Chim and Pumbu, who both sit down again, obediently resuming their nesting positions by his side. And then he looks to me, and in his stare, his eyes, there is less disappointment now and more determination – that even though I might be right that we should leave, I must, first and foremost, respect his decision as my father and group leader.

And so I turn and walk slowly away, the clouds suddenly very dark as the storm breaks.

part **3**

23

When we finally stop walking I am tired. We have come to a guerrilla camp, one I have not been to before.

I realise who they have taken me to as soon as I hear his voice, that voice which is so deep, like a giant boar's. 'I knew you would come back to us,' Commander Kalango says as he sees me, and I stare down at his big leather boots, which are still as black as the night. 'This one was a good fighter, he was brave, I am pleased to have him back. We will not kill him, but he must be punished first. He should not have fled like he did. Put him in solitary.'

I hear another familiar sound at this moment, that high-pitched laugh which sounds like a hyena, then feel a hand smack my back, which makes me fall forward onto my knees. 'Good to have you back,' Kola hisses. 'Come with me!' He lifts me to my feet, tugs at the rope tied around my hands, and leads me off like a dog.

'Go easy on him,' the gold-toothed Senior says coolly, spitting out the stick of sugar cane in his mouth. 'We just killed his parents.'

'I will, Koffi, I will,' Kola grunts, and as I am led away I say this name in my head a few times, 'Koffi, Koffi, Koffi.' I must not forget it. One day I will have my revenge.

∞

When I am let out of solitary after five days I must be the Commander's escort again. Even though I do not want to help him, this man who likes to kill and rape, I have no choice.

He is even more vicious than before, and his moods are very up and down. One minute he is telling me he 'loves' me 'like a son', stroking my cheeks with his giant hands which still feel like dried, cured meat, the next he is telling me I must be as ruthless as him and that if I am not, then he will kill me.

The Commander used to drink a lot of pombe, but now it seems he drinks even more. He often has trouble speaking, and slurs his words. He says a 'bloodbath is brewing in the country' and we must be ruthless and kill as many as we can, we must 'chop and butcher', be 'as strong as gorillas'. He also does more sumu, making a cross with sticks, then getting all of us to stand in a circle and watch him slaughter a goat. He eats the animal while it is still alive, chanting the names of the men he wishes were dead, and tells us that these men will be dead by the morning because of the spell he has just cast on them. Why does he not put a curse on the President then, so we can stop fighting once and for all?

I see Lydia again. She remains one of the Commander's wives. He continues to tell her that she is ugly, while Kola taunts her, saying she looks like a boy. She has grown thin. The Commander's first wife treats her very badly, and has told everyone that Lydia has the disease, is suffering from AIDS. She makes her fetch water in the middle of the day, when the sun is at its hottest, not letting her go in the early morning or evening when it is cooler, and she makes her do this with no shoes on. Her feet are bloody and bruised. And when she refuses to go, because she is in too much pain, the Commander's first wife beats her, giving her one hundred canes. She is often beaten until she is unconscious.

We start to drink pombe before we go into battle. 'It makes us braver,' the Commander insists. We are also given pills to swallow, I do not know what kind, but they make everything go fast, even my heart, and make me feel really angry. Captain Djeke says they are like qat, but more powerful. Whatever they are they make me want to go and kill, and they make me think about it less when I do. They make me believe in nothing, make me feel like just blood and bone, a big piece of meat.

But the day after I always feel on edge, and worry that I am becoming as bad as the Commander and Captain, these two men who have been guerrillas for too long, who now know of no other way to live than to fight and kill.

When we are not fighting government soldiers the Commander takes us monkey-hunting. He says we must 'kill the monkeys like the chimpanzees do, just grab them and smash their skulls with rocks.' But they are very fast and difficult to catch. It is easier to simply shoot them. He also promises us that 'one of these days we will kill gorillas'. He is obsessed with doing this, keeps on shouting about it now, about how 'the silverback' will make him 'strong, invincible'. I think he wants to eat one. He likes to eat what he kills, he enjoys it more.

This day comes sooner than I thought it would. It is raining heavily. We come across some dung. The Commander kneels down, takes some of it in his hands, sniffs it, then rolls it in between his fingers. 'Gorilla,' he finally says. 'We are not descended from them, these big and ugly and dangerous beasts that deserve to die. We are descended from God!'

'Don't we need dogs to hunt them?' Kola grunts.

'No, we're not poachers. We're guerrillas!' he shouts.

Eight of us follow the Commander for many hours in the pouring rain, he is sure there is a whole group of them close by. We get to the point where we think he will never find them, before he finally does...and it is the biggest one he stares at, and for the very first time I see a look of terror in his eyes. I never thought that I would see him scared. He does not reach for his machete, but rather his handgun...

24

The rain tumbles down; it does not relent. The forest is hazy, saturated, obscured by the downpour, and during those brief periods when the rain abates, steam rises from the canopy, the thick dense jungle within giving off a great heat.

We hear an unfamiliar sound, and my father rises. He arches his great back, its silver fur catching the light, which almost seems to make it glow brightly like a giant leaf wet with dew at sunrise, then digs his knuckles into the ground, his arms erect, shoulders tense, head held high and alert.

I look at his lips, which are compressed, then watch him as he stands up and beats his chest, this great rondo of pok-poks resounding throughout the forest. I hoot and chest-beat also, as do two other young males in the group, but we fail, even collectively, to make an equivalent impression.

My mother pulls Lisala close to her chest. My father looks to his left, next his right, then lowers himself onto all fours once more. Other females and children in the group scurry behind him, to where my mother and sister are.

I stand beside my father, a few feet back from him, as does Kibu.

And then there is a sudden explosion of noise, and I see my father rise up again, beat his chest, roar, then charge, his knuckles thumping the ground, bulldozing through foliage, and his screams high-pitched, possessing a deafening intensity, as he opens his mouth wide and bares his enormous canine teeth, the hair on his head crest erect.

The last time I had seen my father so angry, it had terrified me, and I realise, at this moment, that the threat posed to us must be from humans: for it is only them that can make him this angry.

I follow my father, though I struggle to keep up with him, he is so fast. The rest of the group are not far behind me.

Then I hear gunshots and a terrible roar…it is him, yes…

Looking ahead I see that he lies on the floor, badly wounded, surrounded by a number of men, one of whom, the biggest and fattest of them, slashes wildly at him with his machete.

I do not know what to do…

Now I must listen to the hysterical screams of my family – they stand behind me and see what I see – as my father battles this man with all his might, trying to stop him, and the rest of them, from getting to us.

The noise my aunt makes, as she attempts to scatter the group, is somewhere between a roar and a scream. Frantically, she urges us to take the flee route, wishing that at least some of us will be saved.

But we do not run, we are unable to … we cannot leave him … and I stand behind a Hagenia abyssinica and pray that I will find the courage to help my father.

This man has underestimated the level of resistance he would meet from him. My father will do anything and everything to defend his family, and even when both his arms are hacked off, still he comes at the man, dragging himself in his own blood across the forest floor, using his great weight to force the man to the ground and sinking his canines into his neck.

Other men are upon us now and it is my mother's turn to defend us. Like my father she is willing to give her own life.

But there are too many of them now …

I hear more gunfire, a high-pitched scream, and recognise this as the cry of Lisala. I swing round and see two boys kneeling beside her, grabbing her arms and legs. She is dead … they must have killed her with a single blow to the head. I watch them as they wire her limbs to two bamboo poles.

There are mutilated bodies all around me, the bodies of my family …

My father is drawing his final breaths as the man he bit exacts his revenge with a machete, hacking at his neck, trying to decapitate him.

And throughout the agony of these final few moments of his life my father has total comprehension of what is being done to him...he is, in your damn words, 'cognitively aware'.

Though I have assumed human language in order to tell my story, it is wholly inadequate at this moment. Your words are not enough, can never be enough, to capture this horror...

25

I watch Okello become sadder and sadder. He finally comes to me at the end of a long day and says, 'I cannot take it any more, Kibwe. Will you shoot me?'

'No, do not say this,' I urge him, taking his shoulder. 'You will be alright, okay.' I would have said to him before that 'it is better to suffer the death that God gives', this is what my father used to say, but I cannot say this now because I no longer believe it.

And yet Okello is desperate, and so leaves me and goes straight to Kola, and asks him the same thing.

'I would, but I am too tired,' Kola replies. 'I have done enough killing for one day. Ask me tomorrow,' and with these words he lights a cigarette, puts it to his mouth, rests his arms behind his head, and lies down on his back.

I should have known how desperate Okello was, what he might do. While I was sleeping, he took my gun off me and shot himself.

When you live believing you might die at any moment life takes on a different face. Dying becomes nothing. Before I became a guerrilla I was terrified when I thought about death, but not any more. It is easy to think about it when you can see no future.

∞

There is lots of shooting and stabbing and killing now, it is like the whole world is eating itself alive. I smoke lots of cigarettes, and though I know they are bad for me – this is what Mr Nankoma says about them – it does not matter. The first one was horrible – it tasted bad, made my head spin and made me choke – but now I like the taste and do not feel bad. The Commander gives many orders, and makes many speeches. 'We are to raid any village we come across. If we meet with any resistance we must just kill. You are to be as ruthless as the Mai Mai. They fight naked they are so brave, have such powers that pangas cannot cut them and bullets cannot go inside them.

'We must sweep away all the dirt and filth in this country, these weak people who will not join us, who wait for the government to protect them, they must be punished.

'And we must not only kill the men we find there, but the women also, we must rip out their bellies and cut off their children's feet. We must make it impossible for them to fight us in the future, we must simply eradicate them all, these spineless cockroaches.'

And after a bit he does not need to make speeches, we just do it, we kill…and I kill, I kill a lot, and try to stop myself being killed. A single blow to the head with my panga is often enough. I do not need to use my Aka a lot of the time. I know that the pombe and pills are making me lose my mind, I am becoming like a rabid dog, feel myself changing, darkness coming over me. I do not cry any more, my chest does not tighten, my head no longer spins with thoughts. I am hard, hard like stone, feel nothing. The only thing which haunts me is the scream of the beast, the silverback, I will never forget this awful noise, it fought to the very end…

There is a madman in one of the villages we attack. He is dirty like a stray dog, has long dreads and big eyes that stare wildly through me when I stand over him with my Aka. We have searched the huts for food, but found nothing. The village is all but deserted. A few dead lie on the ground. 'Leave them for the animals!' I hear Koffi shout.

'Look, I am a sick man,' the madman says to me, his face thick with sweat, 'a sick African, a victim of war, all my family and friends are dead. Does a man remain a man after so much suffering? I have nothing. I was like you, boy,' and he points at me with his middle finger, 'but I did too much killing. And now I am lost in Lucifer's world.'

I do not shoot him, but leave him be. I think that I, like him, have crossed over to the other world, to hell, and that I will never be able to come back.

But it no longer matters, as God has gone. Were He still here He could not let this happen, no.

⚭

It is not long before the government soldiers come for us, and because we have killed so many people these past few weeks there are many of them. We see the first of them arrive in a battle wagon, a 4 x 4 with the cabin sawn off and a PK mounted on the back. They cannot see us through the thick bush, and we creep up on them.

Before the gunner has time to swing round and fire at us I shoot him, hitting him in the cheek, and he falls out of the side of the wagon. Koffi and Kola do not hesitate. They run round to the front and fire through the windscreen, killing the driver and another soldier seated next to him. Next they jump onto the bonnet. Koffi shoots another two soldiers in the back, emptying his whole magazine, while Kola starts kicking in the windscreen. Glass flies everywhere, and one piece hits my forehead. I put my finger to it and notice that I am bleeding. I look down at the jagged piece of glass by my feet. I pick it up and put it in my pocket. Kola jumps off the bonnet, swings round and fires into the side of the wagon with his PK, screaming madly, bullets punching through its metal sides, empty cartridges filling the potholes in the road.

Suddenly, there is stillness. The shooting has stopped. Kola drops his PK and Koffi flips open the bonnet. We have run out of water, are very thirsty, and so drink from the wagon's radiator. This water is sterilised, which means it is safe and will not give us runny shits. We gulp it down, taking big swigs, until our tummies are bloated.

We hear the whirl of a helicopter, an army Gazelle. The Commander takes me by the shoulder and says, 'I want you to shoot it down,' handing me an RPG.

I remember when I first saw a heli, it scared me a lot because it was so big and noisy, and I hid my head under cassava leaves. It sounded like a giant man who was out of breath, puffing out air very quickly, phwww-phwww-phwww-phwww-phwww. But I am not scared at this moment as I put the RPG on my shoulder and wait for the white light to go on. Though I have not used one since my training, I remember that I cannot fire until the second light goes red.

The heli is in my sights. I see the gunner in the back taking aim. I fire, hear a rattling sound. The heli banks to the right, the rocket misses it by a long way and just clatters to the ground. It does not explode. I re-load and fire again. The heli throttles up into the sky, the pilot sensing the danger, and the rocket clips its side but does not detonate.

More government soldiers appear at this moment, hundreds of them, as if from nowhere, running towards us, their bullets ripping through the trees. We turn and run, back into the thick of the bush, in and out of trees, and I stay by the Commander's side.

I hold my Aka over my shoulder and fire blind.

We keep going.

I hear someone crying, look over and see that it is Kisunga. He lies on the forest floor behind a wall of eucalyptus trees, covered in blood, and surrounded by dead men, all guerrillas.

'Cunts! They've surrounded us,' the Commander shouts, and at this moment a grenade explodes just a few feet away.

I am thrown backwards, everything is black, then I open my eyes to find myself lying next to Kisunga.

I look at his face first, then move my eyes down his body. The government soldiers have cut the inside of each of his legs, slicing from the knee all the way up to the groin. Flesh hangs from them, it looks like meat. I cannot bear to see him like this. He is dying.

'Kill me, Kibwe, please,' Kisunga mumbles through his bloody mouth.

And I know that this is what I should do ... and I do it.

I cannot see the Commander. Death is everywhere, its heavy smell very strong, seeming to turn the air solid as I start to run.

There are lots of guerrillas, most of them dead, sprawled out on the ground like butchered animals. I wonder where Koffi is.

I find him lying against a tree trunk, his legs slashed like Kisunga's. His eyes are closed, but he is still breathing.

A stick of sugar cane still hangs from the corner of his mouth.

This is my chance to take revenge, I think. But I have done enough killing.

Next I am back at our camp. It has been ransacked and everything burns, the government soldiers have set light to it.

I grab a few things...a cooking pot, a small bag of groundnuts, a blanket...throw them in a rucksack, and check to see that I still have the piece of glass from the broken windscreen.

Then I take off my green trousers and gumboots, and put down my Aka. I keep my panga, however. A porter lies dead underneath a lean-to. He is not much younger than me. I remove his shorts, put these on, and also take his sandals. I must not look like a guerrilla.

There is another road near here. If I can get to it, then I might be able to jump on one of the banana trucks heading south.

I see some government soldiers ahead. If they see me they will kill me. I must hide.

I climb a tree, sit on one of its branches, and wait. I do not move again until it is sunset and I can no longer see the big red sun.

I have to run fast, I know this, get out of the bush before it is night, otherwise I shall never find my way to the road.

As I run, I hear the voice of the Commander in my ear shouting, 'Rip out their bellies!' And now I see these cut bellies all around me, bloody and gooey insides trailing to the ground like loose vines, and I must scramble through them, tripping and slipping, and as I do I hear the cries of Kola calling after me, shouting, 'Cut them! Slice them! Kill them!' But when I do not stop he shouts something different, and is joined by the Commander: 'Coward! Cockroach! We're going to cut you up!' And though part of me senses that everything I am seeing and hearing now is not real – for they are not behind me, they have either been killed or escaped – I still believe in it all, am still very scared, and so keep running until I have such a bad stitch that I just cannot run any more – it is like there is something inside me trying to prise me apart – and then find myself falling and falling, sliding down a muddy slope, into the blackness, until I am on flat ground.

I lie on the road, I have reached it just in time, and hear the throb of an engine. It might be a battle wagon full of government soldiers? But then, if I do not try and flag it down I will never get out of here. I take a chance and hurry into the middle of the road as the engine gets louder as it nears me. The glare of the headlights means I still do not know what vehicle it is. I just stand there, waving my arms. It comes to a halt, its brakes moaning and screeching.

'What are you doing, boy?' I hear a voice call to me.

I put my hand over my face to shield my eyes from the glare of the headlights and walk slowly towards the vehicle. It is a banana truck, and at least ten people sit in the back, perched on a mountain of fruit.

'I need a ride.'

'Get in,' the driver says. He has a round face and fat cheeks.

A hand comes down and helps me climb into the back. I bury my legs in between a load of big bunches.

I am not sure where I am going yet, but what I do know is that I want to get as far away from the fighting as possible.

As the wind blows across my cheeks I start to think about going deep into the forest, the part of the forest I have never been to but which my mother described to me so vividly. There are no people there.

I want to go there. For I have had enough of people.

26

I do not stop... I just keep on moving.

I have no idea where I am going, but it does not matter.

Days have gone by, weeks, I have continued moving, deeper and deeper into the forest... to a place where I am sure I will never encounter man again.

It is getting dark. I hear whimpers, but also grunts and barks and growls. I move closer to these noises, and see two golden cats standing over a young bushbuck, who lies sprawled on the ground, their heads buried in her side.

Suddenly the whimpering stops, she must have died. They gorge on her, scooping out gobs of guts. I hear her flesh ripping.

But then I realise she is still alive as her head twitches.

I want to chase off the golden cats. I might be able to save her, I think. But then, these golden cats did not kill her like the guerrillas killed my family, for the sake of killing. Rather, they killed her because they must eat.

I wonder how they got to her. She must have been weak or lame. One of the golden cats looks at me, his face thick with her blood, then returns to his meal. He continues to eat furiously, aware of nothing else. I know they will consume every bit of her, even her bones and hide.

I hurry on, longing to hear my father's belch-grunt, and eventually find a place to sleep for the night. I do not bother building a nest.

Lying here, I cannot sleep. I hear vocalisations... they sound like Lisala's, her loud play chuckles...then I hear more, the pig-grunts of my mother, the hootseries of my father. They are still alive, yes. I get to my feet and run in their direction...the noises get closer...I am near...I long to see their different noseprints, their different faces.

But all of a sudden I hear nothing, everything is silent...and I realise that I am just imagining. They are not close by, they are not vocalising, they are dead.

I can sleep for no more than a few hours at a time, and it is the memory of their murder which I always wake to. I do not wish to think what they have done with my father's dead corpse. I am sure that you, dear reader, are familiar with at least some of the grisly gorilla memorabilia on offer, sometimes referred to as 'trophies', which include hands and skulls. Some humans still believe that the consumption of various parts of a silverback – a concocted brew of his ears, tongue, small fingers and testes – leads to increased strength and virility, and hence the prices paid on the black market are high: the trade in my species' body parts is big business – we are now food for the urban rich. I pray that my father's dead body has not suffered such a mutilation and exploitation.

Anti-poacher patrols had increased, when there was a brief ceasefire, but the resumption of fighting saw them decrease once more: when *you* humans must battle for your survival, any other species becomes expendable. In fact it is extraordinary what atrocities you will commit when you judge your survival to be threatened. I can offer you no respite from the idea of ineluctable human aggression.

I am angry with my father, angry because of his years of goodwill and optimism. Yes, he might have become cynical of humanity towards the end, but he should have been sceptical from the beginning, for then he might not have insisted that we stop fleeing and stay put, close to them, in the hope that they, humans, might finally grasp their ignorance and delusion and treat us, their ancestors, and the rest of the animal world – to which they belong – with care and concern, not cruelty and indifference.

I groom myself intensely. How I long to be groomed by another. I miss them so much.

part **4**

27

The truck stops at a checkpoint, which consists of nothing more than a couple of young government soldiers standing by an old oil drum. They are drunk and high. I know this instantly from the way they move and the red in their eyes. They wear a mix of civvies and uniform. I am worried they will recognise me as a guerrilla, and arrest me, even kill me. But how can they know that I was one? They cannot, I tell myself, and make sure I say this in my head a few times to make myself feel safer.

They want to know where we have come from, and ask us if we have money. Some government soldiers, like some policemen, are like this, they are corrupt. One man gives them some, saying, 'This is from all of us.'

This is very kind of him. I was worried what I would do if they asked me. For I do not have any money.

They let us drive on, and we travel for many hours before we stop.

A few of the people on the back get off to go to the toilet. Though I need to as well, I do not, because I am worried I will lose my place. Like me there are others looking to hitch a free ride, and they know that if the fat-cheeked driver is able to he will also make room for them. He is a good man, I can sense this.

When we get moving again I soon fall asleep, my head full of the dreams of the deep forest, and when I finally wake up – the driver leans over me, shaking my body from side to side, as if I am a floppy dead goat – I am the only one left. Everybody else has got off. I must have slept for a very long time. He says to me, 'This is it, my friend. I am not going any further.'

'Thank you,' I reply, rub my eyes, and clamber to my feet, stumbling on bananas as I do. It is early morning.

'Take these with you,' he says, and hands me a big bunch.

I smile at him, then walk away.

After so many hours on the back of the truck my bum is numb, so numb that when I touch it I cannot feel it, like it is no longer there. I am desperate to relieve myself. I piss by the side of the road, then start walking, I do not know where to.

At midday I come to a fish market, which stands on the side of a huge river. It is dirty and rundown, with lots of tin huts, the smell of fish thick in the air, so heavy it almost makes me choke. There are lots of different voices here, people from all over Africa, maybe all of them running away from something, like me.

There is a church not far from the market, I hear the sound of worship, people shouting and singing the Lord's name. It is only men who work here, it looks like. The women I see are just standing in line to buy fish. They wear colourful filthy dresses.

I watch fishermen climb out of their boats and wade through the water to the riverbank. They get up very early to go fishing, I was taught this at school, sometimes as early as three o'clock in the morning, and they must be tired. It is a hard life, but not as hard as the life of a guerrilla.

The sound of talking and laughing. I look round to see people walking out of the church and heading towards the market. It will be busy soon, full of worshippers wanting to buy fish after giving themselves to the Good Lord. They sell raw and cooked fish here, I have eaten just bananas the last few days, and fancy some. And because I know I want to get far away from people, it does not matter if I steal some, I say to myself. How can I worry about doing this when I have killed people, which is far worse.

I go and stand by one stall. The man here is very busy and has lots of customers. He shouts prices at them, then bags the fish and takes their money. I wait till his back is turned and, as he takes one large fish from the table behind him, I grab two small smoked ones which hang from the front of his stall and run. He does not see me, but one of his customers, a middle-aged man, does, and shouts, 'Thief!'

Almost immediately this man's feet and breath are behind me. Next I hear the feet of others, who must have joined him. I look round. There are at least five men running after me. I hope that none of them are good churchmen. Though the bush has made me fit and I know they will not be able to keep up with me – I am too fast and nimble for them, these men are all a lot older than me – I wonder what they might be able to do with God on their side. But then, after what I have seen and done, I do not think that God exists any more. The men soon stop running.

∞

I make the fish last for a few days. I know the forest is still far away and that I must ration myself. I become filthy, I do not wash, my hair wild and matted and locked, but I do not care. Whenever I come across people now I find that they look at me in a funny way, with their mouths wide open, like they know I was a guerrilla who did very bad things. I suppose I am different after all that I have done, and deserve to be looked at in this way.

The bad thoughts are coming back, making me feel very ashamed, and my mind seems to be going faster and faster. I find that the thoughts are not as bad and painful when I am on my own, away from people. And so I start hiding from passing cars and stay away from towns and villages. But soon I realise that even this is not enough, that I must hide myself even more. And so I decide to start travelling by night rather than by day. I will be invisible. It is easier for me to forage for food when it is dark, when no one can see me. I hunt out fields of sweet potato, cassava, any root vegetable, and on my hands and knees, trawling through ditches of thick earth, I dig with my hands, filling my rucksack with vegetables, then run as fast I can, for a number of kilometres, until I find a place where I know it is safe to make a fire out of thornbush or some other dry leaf or branch, to cook, then to eat. I cook as I did in the bush, make sure that there is little smoke and that it does not rise. I do not bother peeling the vegetables, I just boil them. And sometimes I am so hungry that I simply squat on my heels and eat them raw in the field, which makes me think of Kisunga and how we used to joke with one another when we were desperate for food. He used to say that if I gave him one of my arms to eat, then he would give me one of his. But we always argued about who would go first.

Getting very tired, I know I must get to the forest soon. It is hot today, the sun burns orange, heat haze lining the air, my head throbs. I look for a shade tree but cannot find one, then come to a stream. I take off all my clothes and stand naked knee deep in the water. I know I should wash, but all I do is find myself staring at the water as it rushes past me. I stand and watch it for hours, it is as if it has cast a spell on me. It is only the coming of night which breaks the spell, and as I turn and walk back to the bank the water seems suddenly to slow, as if the whole stream is breathing a giant sigh.

I need to find food again. I come to a small village and start ferreting through some rubbish bags like a rat in search of his next meal. I find a can of beans in tomato puree and a packet of milk powder. I take both and run, and do not stop until I am at least half a kilometre up the road. I settle down underneath a big tree, pull out my pocket knife and prod away at the top of the can with the sharp end until I can get my fingers underneath the lid and wrench it off. There is some mould on top, the can must have had a small hole in it. No matter. I scoop the mould off with the tips of my fingers, and eat. The milk powder is out of date, but I do not care. I am too tired to boil up some water so I just lie on the ground on my back, pour some powder into my hand and lick my palm like a weary cat. Then I scoop up leaves until I have covered my body with them, and dig my fingers into the dirt and mud, feeling its cooling, everything silent, ants and grubs on my face and in my ears. But they do not stop me falling asleep.

∽

As the days go by and I keep on walking I start to pass by more patches of dense forest. The land is changing, becoming greener, lusher. I love to walk through corridors of big trees, their leaves and branches often so still in the cool early morning, and listen for the calls of the different birds. But I usually hear just one, a loud whistled note repeated again and again, a bulbul, I think, but I am not sure. Every five kilometres or so I come across a small village, nothing more than a few round mud huts with sagging palm frond rather than grass roofs, which glint a violent green in the sun. I sense I am getting closer, there are more and more palm trees.

I come to a small town that is derelict. A victim of the war, it has just a few brick buildings housing shops with nothing to sell. A few old men sit outside one of them, a rundown snack bar. They are drunk on liquor, it oozes from their breath and skin. They stare at a mad boy lying naked in the dirt and rain laughing to himself. These men have the look of those who have been broken, who have simply suffered too much. I wonder what they will do when the liquor runs out. How will they cope then?

A bit further down the road I pass by a small medical centre. Two young girls with the disease beg for medicine to make them better, while an older man lies on the ground, it looks like he is dying from malaria.

As it starts to rain I come to an old church. It looks abandoned, and I go inside. There are not many pews left, and those that are still there are on their last legs. The pulpit still stands, and Jesus leans over it. He has been pulled off the wall, and off his cross, and put by the pulpit instead. One of his arms is missing, it lies on the altar. The wind whooshes around inside. I do not want to stay here, and so go out into the rain once more.

Leaving the town I come across an old burnt-out car on the side of the road. It has no wheels and its inside has been stripped bare, but it will provide me with shelter for the night and keep me out of the rain.

∽

The next morning I finally come to the deep forest. I do not enter right away, but stop and peer into it. It seems to go on forever. Perhaps it has no end.

Then I take my first few steps…into this black green world.

As I walk further inside it gets thicker and thicker, darker and darker. Fronds and branches scratch my arms, and vines and creepers entangle my legs, but this does not bother me. My skin is hard, no longer soft, after years in the bush.

The air is wet and thick and hot. The whole place is steaming. My clothes start to stick to my clammy skin. I realise that I could lose myself in here, simply disappear. For the first time in ages my thoughts begin to slow.

After a few hours I sit down to rest by the side of a tree, and it is then that I see it, the beast, for the first time, and it looks a lot like the one that the Commander killed, the one that made the awful scream. And I remember, at this moment, the young one as well, that we wired to the bamboo by its arms and legs, and carried off.

Its head is massive, maybe three to four times the size of mine, and its fur is as black as coal as it stands against the bright green of the bush, giant vines and leaves surrounding it, it seeming to wear them like a great big cloak, and the forest looks so green because the sun is shining now after all the rain, making the whole place glow like heaven – though I no longer believe that there is such a place. It also has a massive brow that goes back and back, and big bright eyes that shine like a jackal's at night. But they look kind, these eyes, kinder than the Commander's and Captain's.

28

I stand behind a huge moss-laden Hagenia abyssinica, obscured not only by the trunk but by liana, which hangs down around me. I sniff, the smell of a male human. I throw my head back, over my right shoulder, pig-grunt, then pluck a few hairs from my shoulder. I am doing this now, I note, this sequence of actions, and feel compelled to do it. Perhaps I am developing a compulsion – a compulsive ritual.

I do not want to engage him. I detected his presence as soon as he entered my territory: we gorillas are blessed with exceptional hearing.

Humans, I can never trust them again. Look at what *you* have done to my kin! It seems you want nothing more than to slaughter us all!

The civil war, which is now raging, is killing us, the country full of Mushamuka's guerrillas and other rogue militias. In fact, it is being reduced to little more than a multi-tribal and multi-national cesspit of poverty and crime, populated by mercenaries, child soldiers, thieves and chancers. Certain areas feel like the end of the world, they have been so corrupted and ravaged, everything for sale, including women and children.

He does not run, but stands still. One thing a human must never do is run from a charging silverback: he or she must stand and face him, though never look at him. I am not sure if he is brave, wise or simply stupid. He appears to be on his own. He is not yet an adult, but about my age.

I stand on all fours and stare hard at him... and it is now I realise it is him, yes, he was with the other boy, wiring Lisala's arms and legs to the bamboo... *he* is one of my sister's killers...

29

The beast looks right at me, its eyes glinting yellow and moving very fast from side to side. I hold its stare. But doing this makes it angry, it roars, wraagghh... wraagghh, the sound low and harsh, its mouth wide open, its teeth massive, and then it charges, its big arms swaying and its knuckles and feet pounding the ground, which rumbles beneath me. I do not know what to do...

I go to run, but cannot move my feet, they are frozen to the ground. Next I feel a trickle down my leg, I have pissed myself. I have not been this scared for a long time and think I am going to die. The beast will hit me so hard that I will be squashed against the tree trunk, and then it will stamp on me and beat me with its fists until I stop breathing. And so I just stand there and close my eyes and wait for it to do this...

But then the sound of it rushing towards me suddenly stops, I no longer hear the great thud of its knuckles and feet on the forest floor, like the gallop of a horse, just the noise of its breath, which is loud and deep, it panting like I do when I have been running hard and need to catch my breath once more. Next I feel something on my face as it puffs out of its nose like an angry buffalo, its breath hot and smelly, and its body odour not unlike my father's after he had spent a full day working the land, rich with soil and grass and sweat. And finally it makes a low growling noise, hurghhh...hurghhh.

I slowly open my eyes, but make sure I do not meet the beast's stare. Rather I bend my head down and just look at the ground. Standing over me I can feel it glaring at me in the hot air, and I am sure that if I so much as look at it again then it will get angry and roar once more. I raise my eyes, still holding my head down though, and see its chest right in front of me. It is bare and black and shiny, it has no hair, just lots of muscle. It is bigger than any chest I have ever seen, the size of the strongest man's in Africa probably, no, even bigger than this, the size of a giant's.

The beast continues to breathe and growl deeply...

30

I am still haunted by what I did...how I froze, pursed-lipped, paralysed by fear, unable to find the courage to fight alongside my father, and then my mother. My whole family slaughtered. I should have been willing to sacrifice myself, as they were. Maybe then some of them might have lived, yes, might still be alive? And I had the audacity to judge Kibu negligent! No gorilla group can survive without its silverback leader. I had watched my father die, and then had run, and had kept on running until I could run no more. How did I so readily succumb to despair?

I bare my teeth at him, and though he does not look at me I know it is he who is petrified at this moment, he who is desperate to flee. Does he know it is me, that I am her brother, that I am now all alone in the world?! I press my nose up against his forehead and breathe deeply, my breath sounding like a muffled, suppressed roar. I feel like an angry buffalo intent on revenge.

Perhaps he has suddenly realised his change in status: from hunter to hunted. And it is not only me who threatens him. Maybe he can sense the few leopards as well, even if he has not yet seen them. Perhaps he has had a glimpse of the fate of his ancestors, who were preyed upon in flat, dry savannahs, living in continuous fear of pack-hunting hyenas, big cats and other predatory mammals. Does he consider me a predator? Well, he would do well to remember that even though I would not kill him for his flesh, I would kill him in order to avenge my sister, my father, my mother, and the rest of my family.

Your subspecies, 'anatomically modern' as opposed to 'archaic' Homo sapiens, has, in less than two hundred millennia, shown itself to be the most violent, warring and patriarchal species on the planet. My species, conversely, one of the great apes of Africa, has inhabited this earth for some seven million years and has been far less destructive.

Perhaps you are simply unable to contain your violence, unable to master this innate destructive drive inside you: for it offers you a kind of liberation. You were born out of such aggression: migrating out of Africa you swept through Eurasia, murdering all other hominid species including the Neanderthals.

In fact, let me be blunt. You have shown yourself to be terribly selfish and malevolent, violent and amoral – to possess little goodness! It seems your biological lot is to seize power by conquering others, even if this means killing your own. You pride yourself on the moral systems you have created, even though these very systems have shown themselves to be desperately flawed, superficial and paradoxical structures. In fact, your morality is little more than a veneer of restraint which lies over your vicious core. In the last century one hundred and sixty million of you lost your lives to war, genocide and political oppression, human aggressiveness the dominant force. And yet this slaughter was not just confined to your own species: you destroyed others as well. Just as you found ways to mass murder your own, you also developed the means to kill other species, and on an unprecedented scale, to the extent that many of these are now extinct or are close to extinction. And not all these deaths were the result of predation. No, far from it, many of them could have been avoided.

I dig my knuckles even deeper into the moist ground beneath me, rolling my fists in the dirt. I am furious. I want to beat him. I can sense his fear, I can smell it…his urine, his sweat. I punch the ground…hard…with all my might. I wish that it was his face I was hitting, smashing.

Pan troglodytes possesses a similar murderous nature. When chimpanzees hunt colobus monkeys, first they stalk them; next they run them down; and finally they beat and bite them so viciously, smashing their skulls, that the monkeys either die on the spot or have no chance of survival, particularly when eaten whilst still alive. Chimps also have a taste for human flesh, and have been known to snatch and eat babies. In fact, they, like humans, murder and eat their own kind as well. Brutal violence, it seems, is a strong part of their genetic make-up, just as it is of yours. In 1980, the males of the Kasekela community of chimpanzees in the Gombe raided the territory of the neighbouring Kahama community: they were punishing these younger males for having lured some of their females away. They went on to conduct a number of raids over a period of months until all six young males were dead, often killing them in brutal ways: they held some down by their arms and legs, and castrated them, squeezing their testes out of their scrotums; with others, they ripped out their tracheas, removed fingernails and drank the blood pouring from the open wounds.

The numerous religions you live by would describe such actions as 'evil' – the chimpanzee does not only kill for his survival, but also for his enjoyment – even though you consider such malevolence beyond the realm of all living beings but Homo sapiens, this primate species alone possessing the sufficient intelligence and consciousness to act immorally. And yet perhaps evil is not exclusive to humans. Other species also demonstrate similar pleasure in cruelty. Look at what a leopard does when it catches small prey: it will not kill it immediately, but play with it for some time.

But what makes you humans even more dangerous is your capacity to rationalise such violence, even though violence of any form should never be rationalised, be it in the name of 'national security', 'national interest' or 'human progress'. You no longer kill for survival alone.

Would I do that?! Would I rationalise hurting him now, would I gain satisfaction from torturing him before I finally take my revenge and kill him? No, I would not.

I continue to breathe deeply, my lips still compressed, the rage still coursing through my blood, the hair on my sagittal crest still erect, as I stare down at him.

Homo sapiens does not possess the gentleness, the benign nature of my species. It seems to me that Gorilla beringei is born with a greater impulse to care. You assume that we do not possess empathy like you do, but you are wrong! Our empathy extends not only to our own but also to other species. I remember when my father released a male bushbuck caught in a snare: he used his canines to prise the wire from the small antelope's ankle, careful not to wound him further. He would have died had my father not come to his aid.

And you believe that you are born to become moral, sure that the thousands of years of social evolution you have undergone have made you better at moral decision-making, have made you more morally good. I am not so sure.

I am about to do something foolish…I need to back off, I need to calm down…I must not hurt him. My anger towards humans has turned to hate now. But hate will not get me anywhere. My father knew this.

Slowly, I turn and walk away, and do not look back round at him as I head for a deep concentration of vines and climbers.

31

Though I am scared, I cannot get the beast out of my mind, and part of me longs to see it again. I do not have to wait long. Just a few hours later it charges at me a second time. I do not even attempt to run, but just stand still, like I did before. I stare straight ahead as it rushes towards me, so big and powerful and noisy, and I wonder whether this time it will not stop because it is going so fast, will just crash straight into me and kill me, smash me with its big shoulders, and so I just close my eyes like I did before, but then try and open them, but it is too scary seeing it coming towards me...

The beast stops just one foot from me, its massive head right in front of my face, as before. I open my eyes and look at it for a split second, it has a scar on its brow. Then it slaps me, swinging its big arm, this arm which is as wide as my chest, but not hard. It is like it does not want to do this, get angry and hit me, and yet at the same time it must defend itself, bluff, try and scare me, get me to go away. I watch it throw its head back, make a quick grunting noise, then pull some hair from its shoulder. It does this a few times. Maybe I should just leave it alone, I think.

Why is it acting like this? I ask. Is it because I am in its territory? It walks away again, but this time not as far. I can still see it.

I watch it for the rest of the day, and slowly realise that though the beast might be fierce it is also shy, almost like Inogo, an albino boy I knew at school, who would always go red in the face when you talked to him and sit on his own underneath a tree during lunch. The Commander said that gorillas are 'big and ugly and dangerous beasts that deserve to die'. But the more I look at this gorilla the less ugly and dangerous it seems, the less it seems like a beast. I do not see a stupid animal either. No, it seems to be wise.

I remember now what Mr Nankoma said, that we are descended from gorillas. It could have killed me twice already, but it has not.

The sun is setting, I must make my bed for the night. I see a giant tree that has a hole in its trunk. I will sleep inside here, in this hollow bowl. I lay down some leaves and moss, which will make it softer, then clamber inside and wrap my blanket around myself. I look up at the forest canopy that spreads like a giant green curtain over me and the rest of its inhabitants, making me feel safe, then close my eyes and fall sleep.

A few hours later I am woken by many different noises, strange sounds that I have not heard before, and even though I lie in the cover of the tree I do not feel safe. Rather I feel like I am being hunted.

I see tiny flashes of light in the dark of the forest, and then realise that these are the eyes of animals. They can see me even though I am unable to see them. If two of them belong to a leopard, then I am dead. A big cat like this will just gobble me up. I hope it is just a lone jackal.

I look up and try and see the moon, but cannot. I do not want to get out of the bowl of the tree in order to look at it, because then I will not be safe.

When it finally starts to get light I get out and watch the moon before it disappears behind the sun. It looks bigger here and is yellow-orange, the colour of the sun. I breathe out steam, the early morning is cold, but soon it will be hot.

∞

Right away I know that I want to stay here and try and become the gorilla's friend – for like me it is alone – even though at the moment it thinks I am its enemy and acts like it wants to kill me. I need to make a camp. I decide to build a shelter like the one I had to build for the Commander. I choose a spot in between three big trees, which stand over me big and tall and make me feel safe, like they are my escorts, protecting me like I protected the Commander. I also make sure that the spot is near a stream, as I know how important it is to have water for drinking, cooking and washing, and that it is right by a forest clearing, in a patch where the sun can get in. I cannot make a fire without the sun. The water here tastes sweet and cold, not like the water I often drank in the bush, that was dirty and bitter. The stream is a beautiful colour, a dark blue-green, full of shadows. I use bamboo to make the shelter's frame, and palm fronds for its roof. I finish it in no time.

I realise that if I am to survive I must be organised, do chores every day like getting water and firewood and food. I must do the job of a man and a woman, because I am on my own. I no longer have my mother and father to look after me. I use my panga to cut down wood and the piece of glass from the broken windscreen to make a fire. I am good at making fire after all my time in the bush, can make one with just a handful of dry grass. I then find a large piece of bark, get rid of the moss that grows on it, and use this to collect food in, like bamboo shoots and forest fruits. I find blackberries and a fruit that looks like a small pineapple. I boil these up in my cooking pot until they become all mushy and make a thick stew. It tastes good. I do not want to set traps and snares like we used to in the bush. We often caught duiker, and sometimes bushbuck. I have done enough killing. I do, however, eat any snails or insect grubs I find. I do not want to eat just fruit, because the last time I did this, when I was in the bush and ate just mango, my stomach rumbled a lot and gave me pain and made my shit runny. It was so bad I made a mess in my trousers.

Every morning I gather fresh leaves and lay these on the floor of my shelter to keep it dry. When I was a guerrilla I would often have to sleep on damp ground and would wake up cold and shivering. During the day I start not wearing my shorts. I wear them at night only, to keep my legs warm. When it is sunny I wash them in the stream in the morning, rubbing them with citrus leaves, which are a bit like soap, then hang them in the forest clearing and wait for the midday and afternoon sun to dry them out. I hang them on a long vine which I have tied between two trees, my very own clothes line. I have only three items of clothing, my T-shirt, shorts and underpants, but this is okay. I wash them every few days along with my blanket.

I like to stand naked in the stream, feeling the air move around my body, and I always stay for longer when I am waiting for my clothes to dry. Because I now wear just my underpants during the day, my legs get cut and bruised a lot as I follow Zuberi. This is the name I have given him, it means 'strength'. I knew almost right away that he was a male like me. I must clamber, like he does, among creepers and broken trunks, and often get stung by nettles and bitten by ants. But after a while I start not to notice these scratches, bites and bruises. My body and skin toughen up. I must look funny wearing what I do, just underpants, a T-shirt and sandals, but only Zuberi and the other animals can see me, and none of them laugh at me, so they must think I do not look too stupid.

Though there are no people here I feel quite happy. I am not lonely, the animals keep me company. They talk to me all the time, making different noises to tell me where they are and what they are doing. They sometimes compete for my attention, cooing, singing, hooting, grunting or growling, and I feel like I am Noah, but with a forest instead of an ark.

There is a magic about this place, and I love its silence after all the noise of war. Everything is giant here, worms that are as big as snakes, and trees that are so tall they seem to go all the way to heaven. This is because of all the rain.

I often stand in between these enormous trees and sniff – the forest has a beautiful smell – then take deep breaths, sucking as much air as I can inside my lungs, filling them until they might just pop like two big balloons. The air is clean, not made dirty by dust from roads, smoke from engines and powder from guns. I also love to sit and listen to the air as it breezes through the forest…past leaves, their faint crackle and rustle, and branches, their quiet creaking and whispering.

I must get used to night-time in the forest, it is as black as Zuberi's fur. I know the dark, know how to make my way around in it – we would often run out of candles or paraffin in the bush – but it is darker here because there are just thick trees above, not the night sky, which at least gives off some light from the moon. It is noisy as well, for this is when the animals come to drink in the stream, and the tembo and buffalo are the noisiest of all.

During the night I dream a lot, mostly of my mother, and the dream is often the same. And tonight is no different. It is me as a small boy pressed against her bare back – she carries me in a skin sling – and I feel so safe, my cheek resting against her back, her skin soft and warm. I remember that when it was really hot she used to put my head in a calabash to protect it from the sun, and this made me feel dizzy, and I liked to lose myself in this funny feeling, just as I like to lose myself at this moment in the memory of it, and the memory of her, my dear mother.

32

He might just be following and watching me, but I regard this as an intrusion. He is in my domain now. He would do well to remember that my rights here supersede his. If he threatens me, I will kill him. And my compulsion, well, it is getting worse because of him. I now have a bald patch on my shoulder.

I rise early, before daybreak. I am eager to travel. The testosterone in my body is running riot: I feel the need to assert myself constantly. My father had his pick of four females, including my mother. They all adored him. I am yet to reach sexual maturity but am not far off now, just a year or so. The hunt for females is on, I know this.

I wonder what I will do if I take control of a group that has infants in it. Will I kill them, as other silverbacks before me have done, and still do? I would hate to do this, to allow myself to be so governed by my drive to reproduce that I do anything in its service, even kill. My father took on two females with year-old infants, but did not kill their young. Rather he simply waited until the infants were older and the females had ceased lactating, and thus were ready to have children once more, his children.

Some of you claim that our propensity for infanticide is proof of our bestial nature: our need to reproduce drives us to kill. And yet your biological drive to procreate also makes you kill. In some tribal societies forty-five percent of babies born fail to survive beyond the first five years, mainly due to infanticide. In both our species, survival – the need to procreate and reproduce – precedes morality. It is only in modern affluent societies that you have become rather more precious about your children.

I was a very large immature. By the age of eight I weighed eighty-five kilos, not much less than my mother: I had an enormous appetite. I realise that I must get this appetite back if I am to survive and have a family of my own. Strength is a crucial attribute for a young lone silverback. We silverbacks are built to fight, to acquire females, to reproduce. Just like Homo sapiens, it is the male of my species who is more predisposed to competition and confrontation. I have eaten little since the death of my family: grief has hit me hard. I would do well to eat lots of fruit and bamboo, and leaves, as many as I can muster: for they are full of fibre. Bracket fungus, which contains calcium and potassium, would also do me good. And I should seek out insect larvae as well, some worms and grubs, as I used to do when I was an immature: I need protein. I got very good at finding them, typically hidden behind slabs of moss or decaying bark on tree trunks.

Though violence horrifies me now, after what was done to my family, I realise that I will most likely have to employ it when I acquire my first mate. The image of my father's final challenger still haunts me: he was made to look weak and pathetic, no match for my father, and though I revelled in my father's victory, I was disturbed by the fate of this lone male, destined to spend the remainder of his days alone, without a mate, without a family. There is a brutal law at work in my world: only the strongest and the fittest survive. And yet the same law prevails in your world also, despite the protestations of Christian and other humanitarian voices, which fall on deaf ears.

I used to be full of braggadocio, always chest-beating and mock-charging. I remember watching my father when he became angry: he would stamp his feet, smash branches, pound his fists. I loved the sound of smashing branches and would often go off on my own to practise: it made me feel strong and powerful like him. Though at first all I succeeded in doing was hurting myself rather than snapping any branches, with practise this happened less as my arms became faster and bigger. I am less interested in such shows now, unless I deem them absolutely necessary.

Like humans, the period of association we have between children and parents is long, kin ties are strong, and thus without them I feel utterly lost. I also miss my siblings and other peers terribly. Though I realise I was very close to leaving my family – I was unwilling to depose my father (even though I was very angry with him for his stubborn decision to stay put) and I was aware of the consequences of inbreeding – this does not diminish my sense of loss.

I watch him now as he stalks one of my neighbours, an elderly female giant forest hog. He moves well for a hunter, he is light on his feet, makes little noise. The hog is, as yet, unaware that she is being followed. He must have found her dung first, and tracked her this way.

He was most likely taught by his father how to hunt. An African cannot afford to be squeamish, he or she is always close to death, yet to experience the privilege of the First World, where death is masked, packaged and presented as if it were life. Here in Africa many humans must still hunt for their food, spear the animal, finish it off with their bare hands, then slit its throat, skin it, gut it, cut it up and cook it. Unless you are willing to handle the blood and sinew of the animal you have just killed, to have your hands full of gore, then you should not eat meat.

I am surprised that he has not set a trap. For this is what his kind normally does. Rather, he hunts on foot. I cannot see his spear or machete. The latter still haunts me, the memory of the blades sweeping down on my father, then my mother, slicing their skin and dismembering their limbs.

Perhaps he has not set one because he is concerned that I might get caught in it. I am now pretty sure that he does not want to harm me. In fact, I believe he wants the very opposite: to befriend me. He still clearly does not recognise me. For if he did he would not be foolish enough to try to make friends with me, surely. I will never forgive him!

I learnt much from my father about traps and snares. After my mother was caught in one that time he was determined to teach his children all there was to know about them: he taught us well. Hence, were he using them now, he would have to set a new kind in order to capture me.

And yet I also sense that he has not laid a trap because he wants it to be a fair contest. Better that he is made to struggle and fight for his food than simply to sit back and wait for it to be ensnared or to shoot at it from a distance. At this moment I recall how I once watched a male leopard kill a female boar, and how the latter continued to fight even when her back leg was severed from her body. She failed to heed the alarm calls of the monkeys above her, who barked incessantly as the leopard came close. He did not set a trap or use a gun. No, he stalked and hunted her. Watching him stalk her was extraordinary, how his body moved, his shoulder blade rising and falling in counterpoint to the swinging legs, this motion so graceful and controlled, even though it culminated in a violent scramble and wrestle of flailing limbs and bloody jaws. And though the killing was brutal to watch, it was also beautiful, a stark depiction of the laws of nature. The leopard killed in order to survive. I did not want to watch him eat his prey, but caught sight of him later, his face and neck covered in dried blood, the blood of the boar.

The boy is close now, almost within striking distance of the hog. Still I cannot see his machete – parts of his body are obscured by the dense forest. He cannot see me. I look into his eyes and see a sadness in them, as if he does not want to do what he is about to do, as if he is fighting against his powerful instinct for meat. I am fully aware that his species struggles without it, especially in the forest: fruits, leaves and berries are not enough. Watching him reminds me of my father, who, when he first lured the two females with year-old infants into his group, did not kill their young but was prepared to wait. He, then, had fought against his powerful need to reproduce. Many silverbacks before him had simply killed without compunction. But how can I be sure that the boy will be able to resist his own predisposition, that he will not just go ahead and kill her, this old hog?

33

This giant hog, it is the size of a donkey. I have not eaten meat in a long time, my body feels weak. Perhaps I should try and kill it. If I eat it, then maybe I will get my strength back.

I stare at the animal as it ferrets, nose to the floor, for food. It is so big that I will have enough meat for a long time. In the bush, when we had nothing to do, we used to make spears. We would find a branch that was straight, break it off the tree, next get a big stone with a flat, sharp edge and use this to take off the bark and get at the wood underneath, then make it pointed at one end, using our panga, making it sharp enough to go through the hide of an animal. But I have not made a spear while I have been here, for I do not want to kill animals any more.

What the Commander did to the pregnant boar now comes to me, how he slit her belly with his machete, her guts and babies tumbling out in a slimy stew of blue, purple and pink. Perhaps I could make a catapult and just hunt birds, I think. But I would need to kill a buck in order to make one, use the animal's skin. I used to shoot down doves when I was a child, my father taught me. He also showed me how to pluck them, clean them, then roast them on a small fire. But I do not want to kill birds either.

I stop following the hog and make myself focus on Zuberi again. Where is he? I wonder. I am starting to learn how to track him. I remember what the Commander did, he picked up the dung and smelt it to see how fresh it was. I do this now as well. It is a bit like a horse's, but for the fact that I find whole fruits in there, particularly blackberries. It does not smell that bad, this must be because he does not eat meat. I find him quickly, he is close by. Maybe he was watching me instead of me watching him.

∞

I keep on tracking Zuberi as the days and weeks go by. I learn to tell the difference between his shit and a buffalo's. The latter is bigger, like a cowpat. I find that it is not that bad to touch. I must do this to feel how warm it is, so I know how close by he might be. But I also learn to tell how old it is by looking at how many flies are on top and how many little white eggs there are. It is amazing how much noise the flies make when they buzz around his shit, and it is like their buzzing is louder than it normally is, maybe because they are so excited.

At first it is very difficult to find him every day, but then I realise I should be looking to follow his tracks to where he is going, not where he has been. I start to recognise his big knuckle prints, and begin to look for bits of food on the floor, peelings of thistle or bamboo, foraging like he does. He is quite a messy eater. I realise he is harder to track than a buffalo, because he does not follow a trail, but rather is always looking for a fresh patch of forest to feed on.

Sometimes I forget to look up, into the trees. When it is sunny he often climbs up one of them and lies on a big flat branch. He uses his arms to pull himself up the trunk, and his big toe like a thumb, using it to grip the bark. When I try and climb a tree I find it a lot more difficult. This is because I do not have a big toe like he has, I do not have as many muscles on my feet, and my arms are not nearly as strong as his.

I discover that there is a large meadow a long way to the south and a small lake about the same distance to the west. But I do not bother going to these places to look for him, because I know he is staying away from them for the very same reason as I am, because there are people there. He needs the protection of the thick forest like I do.

His muscles seem to get bigger day by day – maybe he is growing like me – and every time he sees me it is as if he has to demonstrate how big and strong he is as he stands on all fours, pushes his chest out, arches his back, roots his legs to the ground, straightens and flexes his arms, and proudly holds his head high, turned slightly to one side, like he is the King of the Jungle. I notice his chest is becoming wider, the main of black hair on his arms and shoulders thicker, and the grey on his back turning silver. He will soon be a perfect fighting machine. If he were a man he would already be the biggest, strongest man in the world.

I wonder why he is so big. Maybe it is so he can defend himself from attack. But which animal would attack him other than man? Another big male gorilla like him maybe. Perhaps Zuberi showing me quite how strong he is every time I see him is not just him making trouble but him making peace. This might sound strange but as soon as I act submissively, show him that I do not want to challenge him, then he always stops his posturing and relaxes.

He sleeps in a different place every night, building a new nest each time. It is always round, made of bulky plants, and sturdy, like what a bird builds, but just a lot bigger of course, so he can fit in it. He curls up inside like a gigantic baby. Tonight I make myself a nest as well. I will sleep as he does.

I sleep well.

34

As I wade through the tall, vivid green grass this morning I notice that he is beginning to arrive earlier, and know this is not because he is getting up any sooner but rather because his tracking is getting better. I do, however, make it a little easier for him now: for I make sure that I nest down for the night closer to him, to where he sleeps, and so avoid sleeping amidst the impenetrable bamboo. I am no doubt increasingly feeling less inhibited around him, more comfortable in his presence.

I hear something, to my right, and catch sight of a large female elephant with her calf. She walks slowly, sways back and forth.

She stops, and looks back at me. I stand and admire her great hulk. I will never understand how such an enormous animal can move so silently. Her calf is very young.

Next she looks at him, and I wonder whether he has seen her. I hope he has. For like gorillas, elephants are fiercely protective of their young, and as he is a human she will no doubt immediately interpret him as a threat – for she did not see him refrain from killing the giant forest hog – and thus will go straight on the offensive.

And this is precisely what she does. She trumpets, pulls her calf close, slaps her huge ears against her neck, then thrusts her chin at him three times.

And before he knows what is happening, she charges, charges hard, from only fifty yards away, smashing through the vegetation, crushing everything in her path, the ground thudding, and all he can do is turn and run – he might stand and face a charging gorilla, but not a charging elephant – run as fast as he can, and she is upon him in no time.

Ten feet from him I hear a crash as she fells yet another tree, but a larger one this time, which causes the forest floor to rumble beneath me.

And finally I intervene, standing bipedally and beating my chest, and upon realising that she possibly has me to contend with as well as him, the furious cow comes to a halt.

She looks ahead, towards the boy, as he continues to run, then looks at me.

We stare calmly at one another, she observing me as if somewhat bemused by my intrusion, then turns round and heads back to her calf.

And I realise, at this moment, in light of what I just did, that he is winning my acceptance – though not yet my forgiveness.

35

I decide that I need a stick to walk with, like when I was a guerrilla and we had to go up hills and small mountains. Having a stick made it a lot easier. So I cut down a mature bamboo stem with my panga and use this. It helps me stop falling over as often, the forest floor is very slippery, but also helps me pull myself up muddy bogs when it is raining. These bogs are even more difficult to get through when the mud is clayey, and sometimes I worry that I will get trapped in them, to the point that I cannot move my legs any more. All this walking is making me very fit, but I like it, the fact that I am always on the move, following Zuberi's trails.

Because I can see that this makes him more comfortable, helps him trust me more, I start to do things like he does. I scratch my head like him, eat like him, sit like him, and make noises like him, even belch like him. And when I do these things he looks at me curiously, as if I am a game for him, his bit of fun. He might at first try not to look at me, pretend he is not interested, but I know he is, I know he likes to watch me, cannot stop himself from looking to see what I am doing. But if I look at him for too long he gets cross and grunts at me like a pig, uggghhh…uggghhh, and when he does this I just put my head down and nibble on a leaf until he stops.

Today I decide to slap my thighs – Zuberi likes to do this – then make hoo-hoo-hoo sounds, thump the ground with my fists, break a few branches and smash through some foliage. He watches me as I do this, nipping off a leaf, holding it between his lips for a few seconds, then spitting it out. It is like he is saying he is cross with me and wants me to stop. But I want to test him, and so carry on. I get to my feet and beat my chest, I cannot make the pok-pok-pok sound like he can, but he does not like this, he pig-grunts, then roars, though luckily his eyes do not go yellow like they did the first time. I should do something else.

∽

He likes to eat from a special tree, I do not know its name, which has big yellow flowers with five petals and narrow leaves. In fact he always seems to smile after he has eaten from it, making a belch sound like he is clearing his throat, then purring and humming, a kind of happy groan. And after he has eaten lots, he rests, lying down and letting out a big contented sigh. Now and again he climbs really high up trees in order to get at the fruit at the top, and it is amazing to watch him do this, his massive body going up the trunk, his giant arms pulling him from one branch to the next, and he makes it look easy. I try to climb like him, but find it very difficult. And when he has picked all the fruit he wants, he sits down on a big branch and eats it all in one go.

He eats a lot, far more than I do, stopping to feed many times in one day. I reckon he spends almost a third of his time eating. I like watching him pull at the long vines that are wrapped around the trees, stripping the leaves off one by one, then stuffing the stems into his mouth. He can fit very long ones inside, his mouth is enormous compared to mine.

This morning I find him quickly. I do not want to startle him, so climb up a tree and sit down on a branch. I try to be very quiet, I am sure he has not spotted me. He comes and sits right underneath me, leaning against the trunk, then barks, this noise he makes rising at the end as if it is a question, a question bark. It is as if he is asking me how I am today. He does not miss a trick, he probably saw me well before I saw him.

I am not very comfortable in the tree, and as I climb back down he stands and looks straight up at me, next starts to strut around the trunk like the biggest soldier I have ever seen. Then he just stands still with his head up, as if he is standing to attention, and he looks like a giant statue, very stiff. I think he wants me, quite simply, to take in his massive size and strength. He stands like

this for what feels like hours, and he does this deliberately, because he knows that I will not come down until
he moves away.

When I finally get back to my camp I am hot and
tired. I take off my clothes and lie on a fresh patch of
grass. I let myself sink into it, it is damp and cool, and I
lie there, letting my skin absorb all its moisture.

∞

As the months go by I get better and better at tracking
Zuberi, and when I am with him I copy him all the time.
I day-nest when the sun is shining, making a bed out of
grass and leaves – I do not use branches like he does, since
they are not as comfortable – and though at first I do not
enjoy sunbathing, I find it a little boring, after a while I
start to really like it. I also climb trees when in thick
forest. Zuberi often does this in order to reach the sun
instead of walking out into a clearing. He is a far better
climber than I am. Sometimes I manage to clamber a
little way up, but never as high as him, and I cannot sleep
up there like he can because I am scared of falling. He lies
on the branch of a tree like it is a great big armchair, his
back propped up against the trunk. He even puts his
hands behind his head, which always makes me laugh,
since this is what my father used to do when he took a
catnap after a hard morning's work in the fields.

When Zuberi nests on the slopes he does this in the
open so he can see what is going on below him. He is

always on guard. Sometimes I pass by him on another slope and then crawl across to be on the same slope as him. I feel very safe knowing that he is below me. I know he will not let anything pass. The other thing I start to do is walk like him, on all fours, as he is more wary of me when I walk upright on two feet. I watch him closely, how he puts his knuckles to the ground, and I do the same, push my shoulders out, keep my arms straight. But this hurts, for my knuckles are not nearly as big and strong as his are. I wish they were.

He seems to like it most when I just sit huddled on the ground and eat with him, chewing on bamboo shoots – the inner part of them is nice and soft – or narrow-leaf fern. Zuberi eats a lot of bamboo at the moment, the shoots are sprouting. The other things he likes that I also try are wild celery, nettles, thistles and blackberries. He often comes quite close to me when I eat, and just watches, looking very happy and peaceful, and making deep humming sounds. Eating with him is the best way of showing that I am not a threat, that I do not want to hurt him.

I watch him get up now, turn around and pull a big wedge of moss from the bottom of the tree trunk he leans against. It is a massive piece, like a giant portion of posho, though not the same colour, but he makes it look as light as a feather as he holds it in his enormous hand, stares at it, then sits down again, puts it on his lap and starts to pick at it, removing the fern, leaf by leaf, and putting each one to his mouth.

But though I copy a lot of what Zuberi does, one thing I do not do is eat my own shit. I do not know why he does this. He leans forward, puts his hand underneath his bum, catches a piece, puts it in his mouth and chews on it, smacking his lips together and making a yummy face like he is really enjoying it. But I do not know how he can like it, how it can taste good. I know that if I tasted my shit it would be disgusting.

And the other things I try which make me feel sick are eating fungus from the tree and soil from the ground. His stomach must be stronger than mine.

∞

It is funny, I find that if I hide behind a tree he becomes very curious and immediately looks to find me, then makes soft belching sounds as if he is telling me he is coming. This afternoon we play hide-and-seek for a number of hours, and he is far better at this game than I am. I start to feel like Zuberi wants to be my friend as much as I want to be his, and I am able to look into his eyes, though not for long. They are a beautiful soft brown.

He starts to become more playful. I watch him lunge at a buffalo, and even though Zuberi might find this fun the buffalo certainly does not. It runs for cover, then stops and stares angrily at him. I would not dare annoy a buffalo. Then he bounds over to me, whacking plants and strutting from side to side.

I love to watch all the animals, and I see many of them – monkey, elephant, buffalo, bushbuck and duiker. In fact, I start to see the same duiker a lot. She is young, I can recognise her by her wet black nose, her big brown eyes and her little white tail, which she flicks this way and that. She makes a particular noise when she is scared, like a loud whistle. All the animals are wary of me, however, which makes me sad. I think they see me for what I am, a member of the most dangerous species on the planet, and so are wise to keep away from me, to be so shy. I realise that if I really want to get a look at them, then I must be patient, I must let them come to me.

36

As the months go by I find that the more he comes to me the more attached I become, until it is I who seek him out. I know that my mother, were she still alive, would disapprove. How can I be so foolish?! To trust a human who was involved in the murder of my family! And yet he – actually, I am no longer scared of him – is not yet grown up, he is young, and there seems to be something different about him, something which I can trust. But I also know it is hard for me to resist the opportunity of companionship because I have been without it for so long and desperately need it. And like my father, I am too proud to group with other solitary males.

I frequently watch him from the trees: it is more difficult for him to see me up here, and I enjoy making him work. Sometimes he will attempt to climb a tree in order to obtain a new view – he is sure that I am off somewhere, in the distance – and yet often this is futile as I am not far away but rather right above him, high up in the forest canopy, and he is simply unable to see me through the barrage of green. I love it up here, in the trees. And it is not just the views that are wonderful, but also the food on offer, the big branches of the Hagenia abyssinica supporting a delectable assortment of ferns, orchids, lichen, mosses and other epiphytes, which taste far better than the tree's long pinnate leaves and garish pendulous dark red flower clusters.

He is persistent – determined to befriend me. Whenever he makes contact with me now he always smiles; his first gesture is one of appeasement. I suspect he is still terrified of riling me again: I wish I did not have such a short temper. But he can also be irreverent, rather than deferential, this as much to do with his age – he is a teenager, after all – as his character. Humans, just like apes, are predisposed to irreverence as much as they are to respect. And I rather like this about him, that he is cheeky. I know that his species, like the chimpanzee, is intensely social. It is rare for one of his kind to live alone. Why is he here? It is not about forgiveness… for still he does not recognise me. What does he want from me? Why is he not with his own kind?

One of many kidogos, he was so useful to his former guerrilla masters precisely because he was just a child. They subjected him to an initial period of indoctrination, then trained him to kill. And like the thousands of other children, after a while he probably fought without inhibitions and killed without compunction, at times casually, at other times as an extension of play. Yes, killing became fun, especially when he was made to do it with just spears and machetes, the old tribal way, no guns necessary. And I suspect, towards the end, he was ruthless not just with government soldiers but civilians also – most kidogos were, and still are.

And yet there is something about this boy which makes me believe he never quite succumbed to the levels of brutality of others, his fellow child soldiers, who hacked off the hands and feet of anyone who resisted. He managed to retain some goodness amidst all the badness.

If he is here, in the forest, because he has indeed turned his back on his own kind, then I do understand why he is so determined to befriend me. I know that humans need interaction just like gorillas do. Were it not for the companionship of the other animals in the forest I would have lost my mind long ago. He, like me, is not designed for a life alone. Solitude is painful for us both.

I find it amusing how he mimics me – he has even begun to walk on all fours – and I play to this right now as I reach for some buds from the Vernonia galamensis that stands beside me. Surely he will not follow suit. He takes a single bud and puts it in his mouth, chews on it, then promptly spits it out. This reminds me of how, as an infant, I watched my mother and father in order to learn what I could and could not eat, and I raise a wry smile. He assumes that I will find him less threatening if he does as I do, that I might begin to think of him as gorilla rather than human, despite the fact that his appearance somewhat gives him away as the latter. If only I were so easily persuaded. But at least he wants to make me feel comfortable rather than uneasy. It seems he is aware of my hesitation, even reluctance, to get too close to him, and thus is patient with me. But he also knows, from previous experience, that if he is to befriend me then it is I who will initiate this, not him.

At this moment we just stare at one another. I remain intrigued by him, this human. However, I must remain wary of becoming too close to him. Though he shows no signs of wanting to harm me, I cannot be sure. His species is unpredictable, I know this all too well, and just like the chimpanzee is prone to cunning and deceit. I should never be as hopeful about a human's capacity for goodness as my father was.

37

I am now able to find Zuberi very quickly, my tracking has got so good, though he does sometimes actually help me find him. He slaps his hands against his thighs – he often does this before he starts chest-beating – and I simply follow this sound to its source. I realise he does this not just because he wants me to find him, but also because he is excited to see me, though he is far too proud ever to admit this.

Now, when we see each other for the first time every day he just stares at me, not angrily but interestedly. He is learning to trust me. I am becoming another creature, who has become part of his life. And so after staring at me for a few moments, he often lets out a deep sigh, then simply gets on with his daily activities. He has learned to worry less about what I might do.

I notice how much we have in common. Zuberi is curious like I am, he wants to know things, and when he is like this he lets his guard down, is less aggressive.

Right now, I pretend to munch on thistle leaves, and he struts over, he is swaggering, then plonks himself down next to me.

I scratch my head, he scratches his. I am desperate to touch him, but he just snaps his mouth open and shut, his teeth making a clacking sound, as if he is telling me that he does not want me to.

But he smells like my father, has a slight smell of sweat, and I cannot stop myself, so reach out, touch the palm of his hand.

It is hot and clammy, like mine when I am a little bit scared.

He immediately pushes my hand away and pig-grunts, angrily, uggghhh ... uggghhh, not ready for this yet, and so I hunch over and hold my head down so he knows that I am sorry, and knows that he is still in control. I must wait, I realise. It is he, not I, who will decide if and when we finally become friends.

I wonder whether next time he is this close to me I should simply hold out my hand, offer it, and wait for him to take it.

I know that he should not really let me this close to him, but I think he wants to, wants to be close to me, because like me he is on his own.

∽

Now I am so close to Zuberi I start to feel for other animals too, and so when some poachers come, from the south – I never thought they would come this deep into the forest – I know I must cut all their trap lines.

I manage to spot most of them right away, and Zuberi, it seems, is also very good at finding them, locating a few as well. I wonder whether he was caught in a trap once, maybe when he was a lot younger.

I cut ten of them, and only leave Zuberi and head back to my camp when I am sure the area is clear.

However, on my way, I hear a dreadful scream, the scream of a monkey, which sounds like a big pane of glass smashing, high and piercing, and makes my whole body shudder.

I start running, back in the direction of the noise, my heart beating fast, until I am standing over the side of a pit, and look down to see a blue monkey with two sharp bamboo sticks through its chest, these sticks covering the floor of the pit.

It is a young male and it looks like he is still breathing. I climb down, sliding down the side of the pit on my belly. I stand over him.

Blood comes out of the side of his mouth, he is dying.

I take his head in my hands, gently stroke his forehead, then twist my hands very quickly, cracking his neck. He does not make a sound.

I feel bad doing this, but know I had to, for him.

As I climb out of the pit I see Zuberi walking away, his greying saddle, in the late afternoon sun, visible against the vibrant green of the forest. Did he just see what I did? I wonder.

Why are people so scared of animals, why must they run from them or shoot them with guns? Why cannot they love them?

38

I make the climb up the ridge until I reach the highest point, then sit down and lean against a large boulder.

The sun is setting, the sky throbs deep red and purple, giving it a darkly beautiful aspect. I thought they would not come this deep into the forest. And yet he has, so why not them.

I throw my head back, over my right shoulder, pig-grunt, then pluck a few hairs from my shoulder. I have not done this, performed this compulsion, for a long time.

He killed the blue monkey, and yet he had to, it was suffering. I must not allow myself to succumb to distrust again. For this will hardly help me.

Has he not shown himself to be different from the other humans, the poachers and the guerrillas – full of remorse and desperate to make amends?

39

I know it is not Zuberi as soon as I see him...he is not as big and not as handsome. He heads straight for me, charging, and I am sure I am going to die...

But then Zuberi comes from nowhere, hurling himself down from a big old tree, screaming loudly. The noise he makes is like an alarm call, ear-splitting and high-pitched, and he makes it about ten times.

He lands right in front of me, his back to me, rises onto his legs, chest-beats loud and fast, then roars, slapping down the vegetation in front of him as he does so.

The other gorilla looks terrified, and there is a strong smell as both of them shit everywhere, their shit loose not firm, like dirty water, its stench hanging thick in the air, reeking of sweat also. I do not want to breathe it in because it might make me puke, but then I cannot avoid it.

Both of them stand rigid, like soldiers standing to attention, legs straight and stiff, heads held proudly up. They do not look at each other. It is very quiet.

I slowly walk backwards towards Zuberi, and the closer I get to him the safer I feel.

They face each other now, their head hair standing on end, until Zuberi goes to walk away but then swings round and lunges, hurling himself towards the other gorilla, who in response just turns and runs, and I watch as he flees.

He does not stop, but just keeps going, and Zuberi keeps his eye on him all the time, and still the horrible smell fills the air.

∽

Now Zuberi stands and struts, punches the ground, pig-grunts, he is angry, pumped up.

I go to touch him, like I want to thank him, but he is frustrated, cross with me, as if he does not want the burden of me, and so does not let me, rather just stomps around, smashing down foliage, beating his chest and roaring, like he is in a big strop.

He finally comes to a standstill right in front of me, breathing deeply, then presses his lips together, creases his brow and slumps on the ground, sitting on his bum and staring at me softly.

Maybe he makes a big display like this when he is challenged in order to avoid actually fighting. If so, then men should do the same, because this would stop them killing.

He continues to stare at me, gently, then pushes me in the chest, as if he wants to play, and I fall back onto my bottom.

I look at him now and he looks mischievous, just like I used to when I was younger and knew I had done something wrong. Perhaps he needs to have fun after being so serious.

And obviously he does, because he then giggles, huh-huh-huh-huh-huh, which sounds like a series of rapid pants.

I think he at last cares for me. He must do, otherwise he would not have stopped that other gorilla from harming me.

40

Thank goodness nothing happened to him: I got there just in time.

I follow him back to his camp and watch as he prepares himself for bed. He takes off his underpants, fetches his shorts from the clothes line, puts these on, then wraps himself in a blanket. Then he lies down in his shelter and closes his eyes.

I wait until he falls asleep, until I hear the rising and falling of his breath, before I walk away and make my nest for the night, which I ensure is close by.

Tonight, I want to be near him.

part **5**

41

There are lots of broken trees and tufts of hair, his hair, I know it is his…and there is shit, it is runny…and there is blood, lots of it. I am desperate to find Zuberi.

I follow a flee route, muddy and worn down by buffalo and boar.

He has travelled a long way, a lot further than usual.

Finally, I see him, and run over.

∞

He is crawling, dragging himself along the ground with his knees, elbows and wrists.

Badly wounded, he has been bitten in the neck…it is deep, and I can see right inside. A fight with another gorilla, a silverback. Surely not the one who had run from him.

Exhausted, he gives up trying to crawl any further and lets his body rest on the ground, a pool of blood quickly forming around his head and neck, as blow-flies gather, buzzing around the open wound.

He makes a moaning noise like he is suffering a lot, and I know I must help him.

I listen to his breath. It is very slow, like he does not want to breathe.

I hurry and fetch water, then make a fire and boil it up. I need to bathe his neck.

Though I am worried what he will do as I kneel down next to him – he is yet to let me touch him, though he has touched me – it does not matter, I say to myself, because he just needs my help.

Zuberi lets me bathe his wound. It smells horrible, is full of pus, and has lots of ants in it, which I get rid of. I clean it very gently, making sure the hot water touches every part, then find some blackjack and put this on carefully.

Next, I bathe the smaller cuts and bruises on his head, back and legs, putting blackjack on these too.

And finally, I lie down beside him and just stroke his head and shoulder, making noises like him that I know he wants to hear, which I hope will comfort him and make him feel better.

42

I lie here in terrible pain, on a bed of leaves that he laid down for me, but know that I will live now, most likely, because of him – for he has staved off the terrible infection that would have spread from my neck throughout my body.

He is asleep beside me, this boy, this young man, who has tried for so long to become my friend, my companion.

I stare at him: he sleeps as I do, on his side, curled up. Next I listen to his breath. Then I look at his body – his torso, arms and legs. Compared to me he is so slender and graceful. And finally I look at his face, the gentle glow of his dark brown skin.

He opens his eyes at this moment, and seems to stare at me – I am not sure if he is still asleep – a soft smile appearing on his face, before he closes them once more.

43

I do this for a whole week, bathe Zuberi and lie with him… and also I bring him food, I know what he likes, and give him new bedding every morning.

At first he does not eat, he is so sick and weak. But slowly, as the days pass, he starts to eat a little, a little more each day.

I would rather just feed him leaves, shoots and fruits, but I know worms and grubs will help him a lot, give him back his strength, and so I collect these as well.

Also, I try and get him to drink water, because I know that when you are sick it is very important to do this.

I make sure I keep on stroking him – he used to do this himself – and it is amazing to be finally able to do this, to feel his fur, his skin, his muscle, his sinew. Other than soothing him, it helps him sleep, and he needs to do this so he can get better.

Zuberi is very strong, and he is soon up on his feet. His neck is healing, though I continue to put blackjack on it.

When I was wounded it took me a lot longer to get better. Gorillas are tougher than people, and are also kinder and gentler.

I notice that his big appetite is coming back, and he eats even more than before, especially fruit.

He starts to share his food with me, bringing it over, though sometimes he likes me to do the work, locking eyes with me and jerking his head back in the direction of the food behind him, as if telling me to go and get it this time.

It is nice to sit with him while he eats. I often find myself staring at his hands, which are like giant versions of mine, except for the skin and nails, which are a perfect matt black, the skin so soft.

I discover that he likes being tickled, sometimes making a sound like a soft chuckle, and in return he grooms my head, picking his way through my hair. He also likes to play with me, often wearing a big toothy grin when he does, and we wrestle and grapple, though he is always very gentle. He knows how strong he is.

I start to think that maybe Zuberi knows my moods better than I do, he is very sensitive to them. I cannot fool him and pretend that I am happy when I am not. He just has to look into my eyes to know how I feel. It is not like with people, who are easier to fool.

When I think of what I was like, what I did when I first saw a gorilla, I feel very ashamed. I saw a young one, no more than five or six, in a small cage in the village. A poacher had her, she was a female I remember, and he was showing her to everyone. Lots of us crowded round the cage, hitting it, shouting at her and laughing. She looked terrified as I leant forward and screamed ha-ha-ha in her face.

Zuberi has taught me many things. I am more patient, more watchful, more loyal...and I am happy again. And the bad thoughts...they have not returned since I have been here, with him, in the forest.

He has got so much stronger, and I notice, right at this moment, that he is again looking down the slopes, as if he is expecting someone or something. He has done this a lot today...

I have the feeling that we are being watched, not by people but by gorillas...a group of them.

44

I have hated him, distrusted him, done my very best not to like him, but it was perhaps always inevitable that I would end up feeling as I do now, so close to him, so grateful that he came to me when he did. Perhaps my father was right in maintaining that their goodness will prevail.

Hanging from a climber and swinging back and forth, I notice my shoulder, that there is no longer a bald patch there: it seems he has also cured my neurosis. I look down at him: he is smiling and laughing as he stares up at me. When I first encountered him he was grim and sad a lot of the time, and so it is wonderful to see him like this, so content.

The view from up here is beautiful, and it is now that I spot her, on the slopes, as I did before, before I encountered her father. She is once again heading towards me.

I had not wanted to come to blows with him, but he had attacked me and I had had no choice but to defend myself. And I fear that he came off worse than I did. An old silverback, he is close to the end of his reign.

Larger than him, I had tried to force him into submission by simply charging rather than biting. But he had used his greater experience, and realising my strength had gone straight for my neck, sinking his canines into my flesh.

I had lost my temper then, and had almost killed him. It was the distraught cries of his daughter that had stopped me. But I had also, finally, found my courage.

He had attacked in the first place because his daughter had shown an interest in me, wandering into my range. A young female in oestrus, her curiosity with a young silverback is usual: she has reached the age where her departure from her family is only a matter of time.

But of course, this fact had not made it any easier for her devoted father, who, though he had known that he must let her go, had nevertheless been determined to protect her to the very end.

She continues to make her way towards me, and I cannot see her father on this occasion.

45

I know it is a female almost right away. I can tell this by the way Zuberi is. He is not aggressive, and he makes a noise I have not heard before, a bit like a belch-grunt, but somehow different.

She approaches him slowly, her stare lingering on him.

They observe one another shyly, before she sits down beside him, inviting him to do the same, then starts to groom him.

It is not long before he mounts her.

And seeing this I know straight away that it is finally time for me to leave the forest, to return to my own kind.

For he, Zuberi, must start his own family now.

∽

God, I will miss him, my dear friend.

46

I learn that her father, though badly wounded, will survive, and for this I am deeply grateful.

I sit with Ayako now, this is her name, and watch my dear friend as he prepares to depart.

The war has not ended, he is not sure what he will do.

I am not sure.

At this moment, he seems to me the utter embodiment of each and every species on earth, engaged in an intense struggle for survival. His species is predisposed to control and dominate, both its own and others.

Perhaps humans must simply impose a tougher system on themselves, which will truly moderate this drive, this will to power.

And if they fail to do this, well then … my species and many others shall be extinct, and very soon.

I will miss him desperately, this boy who is now a young man.

A heavy monsoon begins as he walks off, down a main trail, and after an absence of rain it is wonderful to see the forest consume the water it brings, drink it in, replenish itself.

Let us hope that humans allow all other life to do the same.

Epilogue

'The great apes are our kin. Like us, they are self-aware and have cultures, tools, politics and medicines; they can learn to use sign language, and have conversation with people and with each other. Sadly, however, we have not treated them with the respect they deserve.'

KOFI ANNAN, FORMER UN SECRETARY GENERAL, WRITING IN THE FOREWORD TO *THE WORLD ATLAS*

'The Whites came with a Bible in one hand and a shovel in the other, to dig our minerals and fuck our women. Then you made us fight your wars.'

GIL COURTEMANCHE, FROM HIS NOVEL, *A SUNDAY AT THE POOL IN KIGALI*

Acknowledgements

First, there are a number of people I must thank:

Carly Morrell, again, for her never-ending support and commitment

Ashley Stokes, for his editorial comments and all-important encouragement to 'go onwards'

Rachael Evitt, for her artistry

Robert Hastings, for his design and editorial rigour

Paul Blezard, for naming this book

Dan Bucknell, for his great field knowledge, and his fight

And the following people, for their invaluable thoughts and feelings along the way: my mother and father, my two sisters, Kal Sandhu, Clem Khaleel, Christine Rose, Ojok Charles, Kisunga, Dan Bucknell, Mary Macgrath des Jardins, Ateh Wilson, Bate Bechem, Oleé Wikam, Lydia Bua, Daudi Tumwine, Joanna Staples, Carly Morrell, Natascia Phillips, Rachael Evitt, Justin Marciano, Julien Hammerson, Danny Hansford, Nick Savva, Mike

Hewitt, Thomas Delfs, Paul Carter, Vera Chok, Tom Clark, Lucy and Edd Atcheson, Saeed Islam, Ed Ripley, and Rebecca Swift and Jess Porter of The Literary Consultancy

∽

Second, I am indebted to the following works and their authors: *Gorillas in the Mist* by Dian Fossey, a very important field study of primates, but also a wonderful account of a human's connection to the natural world, and specifically, to the gorilla; *The Human Story* by Robin Dunbar, a concise, brilliant book which gave me some valuable insights into human evolution; and *Our Inner Ape* by Frans de Waal, a compelling examination of the best and worst of human nature in the light of our ape inheritance

∽

And finally, let me also acknowledge some other books: *The State of Africa* by Martin Meredith, *The Graves are Not Yet Full* by Bill Berkeley, *Aboke Girls* by Els Temmerman, *The Origin of Species* by Charles Darwin, *The Zanzibar Chest* by Aidan Hartley, *A Sunday at the pool in Kigali* by Gil Courtemanche, and *Tarzan of the Apes* by Edgar Rice Burroughs.